THE LOTUS HOUSE

THE LOTUS HOUSE

a novel by

KATHARINE MOORE

ALLISON & BUSBY
LONDON · NEW YORK

First published 1984
by Allison & Busby Limited,
6a Noel Street, London W1V 3RB, England,
and distributed in the USA
by Schocken Books Inc.,
200 Madison Avenue, New York, NY 10016

British Library Cataloguing in Publication Data

Moore, Katharine
The lotus house.
I. Title
823'914[F]   PR6063.06/

ISBN 0-85031-602-2

Set in Times by Falcon Graphic Art Ltd, Wallington, Surrey
Made and printed in Great Britain by
Billings and Son Ltd, Worcester

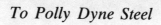

To Polly Dyne Steel

CHAPTER ONE

OLD MRS SANDERSON stared down at a house agent's photograph of "a most desirable period property, ripe for modernization and offered at a bargain price for a quick sale, the owner now living abroad". As she looked it ceased to be a rather blurred picture of a square, gaunt, blind building and became alive, each window crowded with familiar faces; trees grew up on either side of the gate and, on the front lawn, a spaniel waltzed around a pony with bags on his feet drawing an antiquated mowing machine. "Why, it's the Lotus House, and I haven't set eyes on it for more than fifty years. Oh, dear, oh, dear, oh, dear," sighed old Mrs Sanderson. It was a house she had known intimately as a child and had loved as deeply, as momentously and as unconsciously as only a child can.

The house had been built in the year of Waterloo. There was a tradition that the first owner had been an East Indian merchant, who had established a lovely dusky harem there, and that it was he who had planted the giant cedar tree that dominated the upper back garden. This tradition was probably quite untrue, owing its origin perhaps to the name by which the house had always been known — the emblem of a lotus flower, the Indian lily, was carved over the entrance — but it was romantically cherished by the large cheerful family living there in the early part of this century.

It was a house well-suited for family life, being neither too large or grand, nor cramped or insignificant. It had a graceful fanlight flanked by Ionic pillars, and there were pediments over the long windows that looked northwards across the heath to the distant trees of the park. The ground on which it was built sloped south, so that the basement was on the garden level on that side, and curving iron stairs led up to a narrow balcony flush with the drawing-room. Twisted up the stairway and along the balcony was an ancient wisteria and, leaning against the south-west end, a large conservatory housed a prolific vine and two great camellias, one white and one red. Every house of character possesses its own subtle blend of scents — from the wood of floor and stairs and panelling, the polish used on these and on the furniture, the faint exhalations from curtains and covers, and all these blending with other scents drifting in from without. The Lotus House in early summer was pervaded by the wisteria blossom and all through the years that particular scent never failed to bring to the mind of Letty Sanderson the visits she had spent there as a child. One whiff and she was back again in that enchanted place which had been for her both a refuge and a revelation. Perhaps this was because on her very first visit the wisteria was in full bloom.

She must have been just eight years old. Her father had been in the Indian Civil Service, and Letty, an only child, had been sent home to England the previous year to be taken immense care of by a couple of spinster great-aunts. The aunts were as kind as possible and she was not unhappy with them or with the governess who came every day to the small sedate house in South Kensington. She did not know she was lonely, for she had been lonely in India; her mother was delicate and withdrawn and her father busy and seldom at home. Letty had been left to her ayah, from whom she had had the same sort of loving protective care as she later experienced from the aunts, but no real companionship. Then, one day, nearly a year after she had come to England, an invitation arrived from the family at the Lotus House, who were some sort of distant relations of her father's. Little girls were not kept strictly to their lessons in those days and so, although the spring holidays were almost over, she was allowed to pay a visit which seemed to her to extend throughout the whole summer, although afterwards she realized it could not have lasted as long as that. Memories of later visits merged with the first, so that there seemed to have been a continual renewal of joyous experience throughout the four years of her relationship with the house and family.

She remembered her first momentous arrival, though, distinctly enough. She had drawn back into the shelter of the musty old cab that had brought her and Miss Marchant, her governess, from the station, overcome by shyness at the sight of what appeared to be a large crowd of people of all ages and sizes waiting to receive her. Then a plump smiling lady opened the door and helped her down the step and said, "So this is Letty — Mary and Selina have been so looking forward to your coming. Now children, take Letty up to your room so that she can make herself tidy, and then come down to tea. The children have their tea together in the schoolroom, Miss Marchant, you must let me give you yours in peace before you have to return." Blissful words — *"the children"* — suddenly Letty felt a warmth she had never before experienced. Yes, definitely and immediately as she heard those two words pronounced she became a citizen of a new world, the world of her contemporaries to which she properly belonged.

In age she was equal to Mary and one year older than Selina, and she slept with them at the top of the house in a large attic room which used to be the night nursery. It still had bars across the windows through which came the scent of the wisteria. The days began with Minnie, the housemaid, bringing in the big brass jug of hot water and setting it on the washstand with a towel over it to keep it warm, though often they had been awake long before that, chattering to each other. Yet it always seemed a scramble to get downstairs in time for family prayers. The father of the family was, on the whole, an easy-going man but he was a stickler for pious punctuality. No one was allowed to be late for family prayers or for church services. The children sat in a row each morning with their backs to the windows so that their attention should not wander; the maids filed in and sat opposite. The mother closed the door after them and took her place before the coffee urn at one end of the table, the father was at the other end with the big family Bible open in front of him. Somehow, the day starting thus with the double sanction of two masculine deities, one above, the other below, gave it a structural security lacking in the visiting child's life elsewhere — then only dimly felt but important if only that it enhanced the sense of freedom that followed.

Set lessons disappeared with Miss Marchant and each day always seemed an adventure, but yet contained within an ordered pattern. With the wealth of companionship available there was bound to be some plan or other afoot. The eldest boy, Edward, must have been about sixteen at the time of Letty's first visit but to her he appeared practically grown up, capable of being wonderfully kind and condescending and at times exquisitely funny. His condescension occasionally stretched to shepherding the three little girls across the heath and through the park and on down to the Thames, to watch the great barges with their red and brown sails come sweeping along with the tide. The child Letty had believed for years that the East Indian merchant's fortune had been conveyed by night to that very same little pier upon which she loved to stand.

Edward had told her it had to be by night because it was all wicked gains got by looting temples and palaces, and probably his Indian wives were all hidden in the barges, too. She always believed every word Edward said, so she pictured a cavalcade crossing the heath in the darkness at peril of their lives from highwaymen, to arrive at the chosen site where eventually the sacks of gold were turned into the Lotus House.

On red-letter days they would even take the little steamer and travel as far as the Tower. But really most days were red-letter days at the Lotus House. If Edward was busy on his own affairs, the twins, Bob and Jack, were at hand, though it was often Selina who invented their games. There was the thrilling roof game. It was possible to get out on to the roof through a trapdoor, and then to creep all round the house along a deep gully and even to wriggle up and down the tiles into the valley that lay between the back and the front. In this game you were either a burglar or a policeman. Letty preferred being a burglar because it gave her time to look about her while she was hiding. It was a strange particular world up there — the tiles, hot in the summer sun which seemed much nearer than usual, burnt the backs of her legs, sparrows flew up, chirping crossly, she was level with the tops of the chestnut trees by the front gates. She would have liked to have stayed up there for much longer but the policemen were on her trail. The boys would not allow Selina to get out on the roof so she had always to be on guard by the trapdoor. They were always very careful of Selina because she was the youngest and delicate, but they let her climb the cedar for the Monkeys' Party game, though it was understood that the safe broad fork between the lowest branches was reserved for her particular use.

The garden at the Lotus House was, for the child Letty, the Garden of Eden, the standard by which she judged all

9

subsequent gardens. Its especial glories were the cedar, the wisteria, the two camellia trees and all the fruit — the bunches and bunches of sweet little black grapes from the vine, the figs and peaches and greengages that grew along the south wall between the upper and the lower garden, where apple, pear, plum and damson trees all vied with each other in delicious abundance. The boundary of the lower garden was the railway and, though their elders might complain of the smoke and the noise (there was shunting on a side track that sometimes kept up a symphony of banging and puffing well into the small hours), to the children the railway was a source of both interest and pride. The boys especially pitied anyone who hadn't a railway at the bottom of their garden and Letty, who at first was a little frightened of the engines, soon learned to look upon them as powerful and benevolent friends.

A stable block housed the old grey pony who mowed the lawns, the carriage horse Kitchener, Bimbo the black and white spaniel and the children's rabbits. Fred the coachman and Chittenden the gardener were good-natured and long-suffering, and let the children do much as they liked as long as they kept a few well-defined rules faithfully. The three worlds of servants, children and parents each had their own rules. They were interdependent within clearly marked boundaries and the citizens of each world knew exactly where they stood. Even when Rosamund, who was the eldest of the family, passed from one world to another at her coming out, there was no uncomfortable undefined period. On Letty's first visit Rosamund still inhabited the children's world, then, almost in a flash it seemed, her hair went up and her skirts came down, and she belonged there no longer.

Rosamund was Letty's first romance; she was built on generous lines like her mother, and everything about her was warm and glowing. Mary and Selina were slim little creatures, rather pale, with straight fair hair and grey eyes, but Rosamund's hair was a rich red brown and her eyes were hazel, and she had cheeks that really were the colour of pink roses. She played the violin but her real passion was for acting. Those were the days of private theatricals and she was much in demand (but she knew it was out of the question to consider anything professional). She was very kind to the younger ones and invented charades for them and contrived wonderful costumes. "A duke is in love with her," Edward told Letty, "he will come and carry her off soon to live with him in his mansion and be his duchess." Letty was not surprised, though she wished the duke had been a prince and the mansion a palace, but she did not want even a prince to carry off Rosamund anywhere. She did not want anything to change ever at the Lotus House. When at night she lay in her bed between Mary and Selina, smelling the wisteria (for in her memory there it was, always in bloom and always scenting the whole house) and listening to far-off hooting of ships from the river and the nearby trumpeting and panting of the railway engines at the bottom of the garden, she felt so happy and so safe that she knew then for certain that the world was a kind place. Yes, she felt the house wrap her round with such assurance that she could look forward to the years with excited trust.

It was not altogether a trick of memory that made old Mrs Sanderson think of her visits to the Lotus House as being always in warmth and sunshine. Winter visits had been rare, as the aunts thought she needed their own special cosseting then. She would so much have liked to have spent a Christmas there, but this had never been allowed and, like most children in those days, she accepted as inevitable the decisions made for her.

She must have been granted one February visit once though, for Selina's birthday. She remembered clearly the drifts of snowdrops under the black branches of the cedar

11

and the dancing shadows on the ceiling from the bedroom fire the little girls were allowed for a treat. She supposed on looking back that the three of them got on so well together because she, Letty, had fulfilled a need in both sisters. Mary and she shared the same birth year. "Why, you're twins," Selina had said on that first visit, and Letty's heart had given a little jump for pleasure and though the real twins, Bob and Jack, had pointed out the inaccuracy of this statement, still the notion that she and Mary had a special bond persisted. They were actually more alike in temperament than the sisters. "I like you because you are ordinary, like me," Mary once said to her, and Letty knew just what she meant. Selina was un-ordinary — set apart by being the only delicate member of the family, subject to alarming fits of asthma, but more so by the possession of a compelling imagination which often left Mary disconcerted. "You never know what Selina is going to be," she complained. Once for a whole tract of time she was a cat, and insisted gently but firmly on eating most of her meals from a saucer on the floor, and at another time, after Edward had been romancing about the East Indian merchant, she was one of his wives and coaxed Rosamund into making her a sari out of an old sheet, and pretended she did not understand what was said to her. But in spite of the inconveniences caused by such behaviour, she was such a sweet-tempered cheerful child, and so patient when ill, that everyone petted her and Letty, charmed by the delicious experience of mothering someone younger and weaker than herself, became the most willing attendant of all Selina's subjects.

This particular birthday was momentous because of one special birthday present — the doll's house. Letty herself had not possessed many treasures as a child; in India they had travelled too often from place to place, and at Kensington there was too little space. Like so much else at the Lotus House, the family toys and games became archetypal for her. There was the rocking-horse, off which she often had to be dragged protesting; there was the huge box of wooden bricks; there was the musical box with its magical brass discs; there was the boys' sacrosanct model railway with its trains, carriages and trucks, its signals and points and home-made stations, with which the little girls were only allowed to play as a special mark of favour and under strict supervision; and, best of all, there was Selina's doll's house. It was a family present: the twins had been working at it in secret for weeks, cleverly constructing it from old orange-boxes. Edward had painted it, the parents had given the furniture and Rosamund the inhabitants. But the peculiar charm of this particular doll's house, for Letty at any rate, was that as far as it was possible the amateur craftsmen had made it a small replica of the Lotus House itself.

On that birthday morning the three children stood in a row and gazed at the little house. There was the door with its pillars either side and the three windows of the dining-room and study, and above them the correct number of bedroom windows and the dormer attic ones in the roof. Old Mrs Sanderson remembered that she had continued to look at it silently while Mary danced about and clapped her hands, and Selina knelt down in front to open it and look inside. Edward had painted the rooms the right colours, white and green for the drawing-room and dark red for the dining-room, but the boys were quite apologetic that the back of the house was just a blank wall and that there was no balcony and no rooms behind the dormer windows in the roof. But there was quite enough reality to satisfy Letty and she remembered how Selina kept on saying, "But I don't want it any realler," and when Rosamund offered to dress the mother and father and little girl dolls like the parents and herself (for she had not had time to dress them properly and they just had their tiny arms and legs thrust through bits of material to

13

make them decent), Selina had frowned: "No, no, Ros, they are Mr and Mrs Golightly and their little girl is called Wilhelmina Rose."

"Where on earth did you get those names from?" laughed Rosamund, and she had hugged Selina hard so that her hair, that still wasn't very used to staying up, tumbled all over her shoulders (old Mrs Sanderson seemed to see her more clearly now than the child Letty had done). So Mr and Mrs Golightly and Wilhelmina Rose became the focus of a whole series of adventures. In due course a cook arrived, a Dutch doll, affectionately known as "Cooksie", whose bark was worse than her bite, and an old gentleman in a black velvet suit who was Mr Golightly's father. He had been an engine-driver until Bimbo bit off his legs one day — an accident transformed into a terrible railway disaster — after which he had to spend all his time in bed.

There was no end to the Golightly adventures that Selina invented, each one wilder than the others. How they laughed at them! Old Mrs Sanderson smiled and sighed. Was that birthday visit the only winter one, then? No, of course not, there was that later one when the ponds on the heath were all frozen and Edward had taught her to skate. She remembered how proud she had been because he praised her for learning so quickly — all in one day — and how, intoxicated by the magic of it, she had gone on and on gliding faster and faster, until the extraordinary orange sun had set and the brilliant winter stars had appeared. Oh, yes, she remembered that winter visit too, but still it was the earlier one she remembered best, and how she had stood there in front of the doll's house "surprised by joy".

When Letty was twelve her parents came home to England and claimed her, and actually she had never gone to the Lotus House again nor seen any of the family. It now seemed incredible to old Mrs Sanderson that this

14

should have been so, but it had come about quite naturally and inevitably. First, she was sent to boarding-school
and her father and mother expected her to spend her
holidays with them, though neither parents or daughter
were particularly happy or at ease with each other. Sadly,
though they loved each other, they were not capable of
bridging the gap left by four crucial years of separation.
As for the Lotus House, Letty wondered sometimes if her
mother had not been jealous at her constant references to
her visits there. At any rate she sensed a total lack of
interest and soon gave up talking of them. She and Mary
wrote for some time but new interests crowded in, and
then just before the 1914 war broke out her father had
died after a riding accident, and the original link between
the two families was severed.

Her father's death and the cataclysm of the war
marked the end of the world of Letty's childhood. Her
friends dispersed, the girls to join the V.A.D. or to take
up other forms of war work, the young men to the front.
She herself was left with an ailing and bewildered mother
and a much reduced income. They moved to a tiny flat in
Bournemouth, recommended for her mother's health.
She heard from her old governess, Miss Marchant, with
whom she still exchanged an annual letter, that Edward
and Bob had both been killed, and that when peace came
Jack had emigrated to Australia. Rosamund, who had
joined an amateur acting group entertaining the troops,
had made a runaway marriage with a Canadian soldier.
Beyond that — a blank. She had thought of writing
again to Mary but the interval from childhood to maturity
had been too long, and with the war in between besides,
what could she say? Perhaps if she had written, thought
old Mrs Sanderson looking down on the dim picture of the
Lotus House in her paper, the memory of those early
times would not have remained so clear. Perhaps indeed
she had not really wanted to write, lest it might blur that

15

bright image with the stark realization of change.

Her mother lingered on year after year, as lifelong invalids often do, and after she had died Letty made a late unromantic marriage with the doctor who had attended her. He was a widower who needed a housekeeper and a congenial companion, and she wanted financial security. Both liked and respected each other and this had ripened into affection, but she could not pretend that his sudden death shortly before retirement had left her shattered. She missed him but, for the first time in her life, she felt free and independent. She decided she would leave Bournemouth, which she had never liked. London drew her and she began in a desultory way, for there was no hurry, to look at house agents' advertisements. Thus it came about that she was staring down at the picture of the Lotus House, which, in its turn, seemed to be staring reproachfully up at her. How long she had been looking at it she did not know, but now she made a careful note of the agent's address.

"I might do worse than find a flat somewhere in that neighbourhood," she said to herself. "It would be better than settling right in London itself, I think, and while I am about it, I might at least go and see the old place again — not of course with any thought of buying it, but I needn't tell the agents that. Perhaps they can give me news of the family, obviously none of them can be living there now. Oh, dear, how long ago it all seems."

A week later she was asking for the key of the Lotus House at the agents. "No, I do not wish to be accompanied there, thank you," she said firmly as she put the key into her bag, "I know the way quite well."

16

CHAPTER TWO

MRS SANDERSON WENT resolutely along streets that were familiar by fits and starts. The memories of childhood were patchy and of course there were many changes, though the chief landmarks — the station, the church, the concert hall · — remained the same and she had no difficulty in finding her way. A general smartening and sophistication was apparent, two or three big ugly self-service stores had sprung up, and squeezed between them were numerous rather pathetic little boutiques, far too many, she thought, to be profitable. Here and there, though, like a vivid flashback, an old friendly shop-front appeared — the fish shop where the little girls had been half frightened and wholly fascinated by the fish-monger, who looked exactly like a giant fish himself, white and flabby, with pale protruding eyes and large sticking-out ears like fins. There was the confectioners, too, of blessed memory, now called the Honey Pot, where she and Mary and Selina used to spend their pennies and where one day they had actually each been presented with a whole bar of Fry's chocolate cream from a damaged package. Such unlooked-for benevolence could never be forgotten. And, yes! there was the tiny corner shop which, for some unknown reason, sold an extraordinary mixture of greengrocery and Japanese vases and toys. This was the child Letty's favourite shop of all. You went

17

in through a bead curtain, in itself a beautiful and exotic attraction, and there were the piles of cheerful oranges and apples and blue-and-white china ginger jars, and Japenese dolls with round black heads and pretty kimonos and gaily painted parasols and, hanging down from the low ceiling, circles of painted glass pendants that tinkled softly in the draught from the open door. The children bought magic packets of floating flowers here that looked like shrivelled bits of paper, but when you got them home and shook them out into a tumbler of water, they turned into lovely tinted blossoms — "lotus flowers", they always firmly called them.

Mrs Sanderson crossed the road to reach the little shop; the traffic was frightening — it was like crossing a deafening tumultuous river, the ceaseless roar and rush of the roads was the greatest change of all from her childhood memories. But she got across in safety and peered into the bow windows of the shop. It still sold fruit and vegetables and the name over the door, Joseph Budgeon, was still the same, though of course the old man who had kept it must have died long ago, and there was no sign of any Japanese goods as far as she could see. She decided to go in and buy some apples and find out who kept the shop now. The thought occurred to her, too, that she might possibly discover more of the recent history of the Lotus House and of what had happened to the family than the agents had been able to tell her, which had been very little indeed — only that the sale was in the hands of a solicitor acting for the present owner, who lived in Australia. The property had only lately come into his hands on the death of his father, so the agents believed. She supposed that this must be Jack's son. She went up the two steps into the shop that she remembered so well. The bead curtain had vanished and everything seemed tidier, and there was a very neat small middle-aged woman behind the counter. Letty made her purchase and

18

then said, "I used to come into this shop when I was a little girl, a long time ago now, but the name over the door is the same." There was a question in her voice and the woman answered it at once.

"That's my old uncle's name. Fancy that now, there aren't many left that remember him. You were living in these parts then?"

"No," said Letty, "but I often visited here. I've not been here since I used to stay at the Lotus House."

"Well, I never," said the woman, "to think of that. It's up for sale now, is the Lotus House, but who'll buy it I can't think; it's in a bad state. You see, after the two ladies left it, it was empty for a long while and it was damaged a bit from the blitz too; not badly, but neglected, that's what it was, and then it was let for offices. But if you're a friend of the family, you'll know all this, I expect."

"No," said Letty, "I lost touch. When did the ladies leave? Did you know them?"

"Not to say well," said the woman, "but after I came here to look after my old uncle and the shop, I remember them coming in sometimes, and when they were leaving for Australia (their brother sent for them, you see), they came in to say goodbye to Uncle. 'We'll be coming back again to the Lotus House,' said Miss Selina, she was the delicate one, you know. I remember her saying it well; 'Oh, we'll be coming back quite soon,' but they never did."

Letty took up her bag of apples. There seemed nothing else to say, but she looked round the shop rather sadly.

"Your uncle used to sell Japanese curios," she said, "I don't suppose you have any left?"

"We stopped that during the war," said the woman, "but I kept a few, not for sale but my uncle being so fond of them — they're in this cupboard." She opened the door of a little corner cupboard, and Letty saw a doll and

19

a ginger jar and a black and gold box and some faded paper packets.

"Oh!" she exclaimed, "Are these the magic flower packets?"

The woman laughed. "Did you love them too? Here, would you like a packet for old time's sake?"

"Of course I would," said Letty, "it's sweet of you." She slipped the little packet into her handbag and, cheered and touched, she faced the hazards of the road again. She went up a little side street she remembered, to escape from the noise. The houses here had all been drab cheap little Victorian dwellings, but they were now much smartened up with pink, yellow, and blue doors and window-boxes, and cars parked outside the minute front gardens. Old Mrs Sanderson hurried past them for she suddenly felt acutely apprehensive. At the end of the little by-way, she turned a corner, and there facing her was the Lotus House.

It looked even more grim and desolate than it had done in the advertisement. A large FOR SALE board was fixed to the broken-down fence which she read painstakingly through from beginning to end, though she knew it all before.

"Why have I come?" she said to herself. "Whyever have I come? It was a stupid thing to do, but all the same, now I'm here it seems foolish to go away without having a look round."

She decided to explore outside first, and crossing the shaggy brown turf of the neglected lawn she crept along the overgrown side path. The first shock was that the vegetable and fruit garden had turned into a council house development, beyond the ragged winter hedge and a dividing fence. Then the cedar tree had gone, or almost gone, for a great stump remained, but round this the snowdrops were all out, not in drifts where the sun had penetrated the dark branches as she had remembered

20

them, but in a huge open carpet. Then with a wave of relief she saw that the wisteria was still clinging to the stairway and the balcony. The conservatory had gone with its vine and camellias, and in its place was a hideous garage, and all the rest of the garden that remained was a wilderness of rough growth, but the snowdrops and the wisteria had given her resolution to turn the key in the front door and enter the house itself. She needed then all the courage she could muster. Rooms had been divided by matchboard partitions, woodwork now scratched and defaced was painted a dark, dull green, window panes were cracked, boards were loose, old newspapers and wrappers strewn about the floor. Grimly, Mrs Sanderson looked into every room, and climbed the echoing stairs to the attics. These were less desecrated than the rest, they had probably never been used by the firm which had rented the house. The bars still protected the windows of the old night nursery and the faded Mother Goose frieze actually remained beneath the ceiling. It seemed to Letty Sanderson that she had been walking and standing and climbing stairs for a long while, so she sat down on an empty wooden box in the corner, and stared through the nursery bars at the fading February sky until it was too cold and dark to stay there any longer — much too cold and dark and dismal.

She returned the key to the agents just before they closed. "I will look at the flats you have recommended tomorrow," she said, "I shall not need this key again." The agent was not surprised. But when on the third day of Mrs Sanderson's property viewing (she was staying at a small guest-house in the neighbourhood), she asked for the Lotus House key once more, his eyebrows went up quite noticeably. "He obviously thinks me a little mad," said Letty Sanderson to herself, "well, I suppose I am, but I just feel I can't go away without seeing the old place again. I expect by the time I move here it will either have been sold or demolished." She had found the flat she wanted the previous day, quiet, sunny and very convenient.

As on the earlier visit she wandered round the garden of the Lotus House first. There were pale buds showing on the old lilac bushes by the stables, now converted into more garages; she picked a bunch of snowdrops and braced herself to enter the house again. She remembered that last time she had not penetrated to the basement. This, of course, had belonged to the servants' world, and as they reigned there supreme, the children had only visited that particular region as guests or invaders. There was a huge lift in the passage worked by a pulley for conveying the substantial meals and massive crockery to the dining-room, and the boys would sometimes be coaxed into working this with one or more of the little girls inside. But it was a game frowned upon by Cook — "It'll break one of these days, Master Bob, and then who'll get the blame?"

Old Mrs Sanderson crept down the basement stairs. The fixed dresser with its empty hooks and drawers and the old-fashioned grate, rusted over, were the only objects left in the big empty kitchen — the scullery, which she never remembered seeing before, had a vast stone sink and a copper for boiling clothes in one corner—beyond was a huge larder with slated shelves and a tiled floor. It all looked terribly dusty and deserted but there were no signs of alien office occupation here, and in the butler's pantry along the passage were two iron bedsteads, a rug, a basketwork chair and a calendar for 1941 hanging on the wall. *It must have been used as an air-raid shelter*, thought Letty Sanderson. *Perhaps Mary and Selina slept here on those two beds*. She could not imagine it — two middle-aged spinster ladies huddling beneath the bedclothes with the bombs dropping all round. No,

22

Mary and Selina were safe upstairs in the night nursery, with the friendly trains puffing and blowing at the end of the garden. She left the pantry and went out into the passage again and there was the old lift still there. She peered into it and saw at its further end a square object done up in sacking. There was plenty of light coming in from the window on the garden side of the passage, and she bent down to look more closely. A corner of the sacking was torn, and what looked like a painted miniature chimney was sticking out sideways. Letty caught her breath and stared, then dragged the object towards her and pulled hard at the sacking; it tore a great rent and revealed a tiled roof and a tiny dormer window. There was no doubt about it — it was Selina's doll's house.

Her first thought was *How could they have left it here?* Then she remembered that of course they expected to come back and thought it was quite safe till they returned. "And so it has been and so it is," said Letty Sanderson. When all the rest of the furniture had been sold up and the office staff had moved in, nobody had bothered about the old lift, indeed it was obvious they had not bothered with the basement at all. With a good deal of effort Letty dragged the doll's house into the open and pulled off more of the sacking. To her joy it seemed quite undamaged. She managed to open it and found even Mr and Mrs Golightly and Wilhelmina Rose and the grandfather and the Dutch doll cook still at home among their furniture, disarranged but otherwise not showing much signs of wear. Mr Golightly's father had fallen out of bed but seemed pink-cheeked and well. Absurdly old Mrs Sanderson could have cried for joy. She knelt down on the cold dirty stone floor and began to put everything to rights until it grew too dark to see clearly. Then she carefully covered up the doll's house with the sacking again and went home. It was too late to return the key that evening, and when she got back to her hotel room she had a sudden panic that she had left it in the door of the house. She dived in her handbag and it was there all right, but in feeling for it her hand closed on the packet of Japanese flowers that the kind little woman had given her from the corner shop and which, until now, she had forgotten. "They won't be any good I expect, after all these years," she said, but she filled her toothglass with water and emptied the packet into it and, lo and behold! the magic still worked, the wrinkled paper expanded into pretty shapes and floated gaily in their small pond. Letty stared down at them. "Lotus flowers," she murmured to herself, "they must be a portent," but she had known all the way back that the sunny convenient flat would after all never be hers. She was going to buy the Lotus House and make it blossom into a home again.

But Mr Donovan, her family solicitor, was horrified at the idea. "An old neglected property, much too large, really Mrs Sanderson, I don't advise it, I don't advise it at all."

Mr Donovan's father had managed all Letty's parents' business, and he had had charge of hers now for many years, and she had the greatest respect for him, but she had expected disapproval and was not too cast down by it. "I intend to convert it into flats, Mr Donavan," she said, "and to live in one of them myself. It is going cheaply, you know; don't you think it would ultimately pay me?"

"It's going cheaply because it needs so much spent on it," said the solicitor. "You will find it is not at all cheap in the end. It would be a hazardous speculation at the best, but for anyone your age, if you will forgive me, it is a great responsibility — I don't like it, I don't like it at all."

"I'm in very good health," said Mrs Sanderson, "and people of my age aren't really old nowadays. You said yourself that I did well out of selling John's practice and that the Bournemouth house should bring in a good sum."

Mr Donovan was silent. He was, as a matter of fact, very surprised. He had looked upon Mrs Sanderson as a sensible woman, a little shy and reserved, rather repressed he had thought, but decidedly intelligent, and now she appeared as rash and romantic and not sensible at all. She had explained that the property had a special sentimental appeal for her, but it was Mr Donovan's opinion that sentiment could easily be carried too far where house property was concerned. However, if she was absolutely determined on so rash a purchase, he could not stop her, and possibly the flats might be made to yield a reasonable return; the house was certainly in a good neighbourhood.

"Well, we mustn't do anything in a hurry, must we?" he said at last. "We'll get a good surveyor first. I know of a thoroughly reliable firm and we'll abide by their decision." Letty went away with the surveyor's name and address but was secretly determined not to abide by any decision but her own compelling urge.

The surveyor's report when it came was neither damning nor particularly reassuring. There was at present no sign of dry rot, but of course with houses of this date this was no assurance that it might not occur at any time. The roof, though needing some repair, was in fairly good condition, but a valley roof was never very satisfactory. Mr Donovan shook his head but reluctantly agreed to forward an offer to the owner's solicitor after a rough estimate had been made of the cost of conversion.

"Planning permission for the necessary alterations should offer no difficulty, I think, as your aim is to restore the outward appearance of the house as much as possible to its original condition."

"Certainly," replied Letty, "and the inside too."

Mr Donovan was not aware of the implications of this remark until they came to discuss the planning of the flats

25

with the architect and Letty refused to allow the spacious living-rooms on the ground floor to be divided.

"It will ruin their proportions," she said, "and the hall must remain as it is too, with that pretty archway and staircase."

"But, my dear Mrs Sanderson," said Mr Donovan, and the architect chimed in for he was proud of his plans, "that is really impracticable — how are you to get the necessary bedrooms and offices? And, besides, no one nowadays wants such big rooms to heat."

"Then I shall have to have the ground-floor flat for myself," said Letty. She had been undecided as to which of the four projected flats she should choose. At first she thought lovingly of the night nursery for her bedroom, but the rest of the top-floor rooms which had been the servants' were decidedly poky and the stairs, too, might prove a disadvantage with increasing age. Then she favoured the basement for its direct access to the garden, but much of this was rather dark and had fewer friendly associations so, although Mr Donovan again sadly shook his head and said she was sacrificing the most financially promising return of the whole project, it seemed that the dining-room and drawing-room (grand and august as she still held them in memory) would become her living-room and bedroom, and she would squeeze both a bathroom and kitchen and a second little bedroom out of the old cloakroom and the study, to the poor architect's distress.

Meanwhile communications were crossing and recrossing oceans and continents. Letty wrote a personal letter and got a friendly reply from Jack's son. He and his boys worked a profitable ranch and had no intention of coming back to the old country. His father, too, he felt sure, had not contemplated returning, but had never brought himself to sell the Lotus House for purely sentimental reasons. Now, however, he himself was anxious to be rid of the property. It would have been different if his aunts

26

had lived, but the younger had not long survived the transplanting from England, he did not even remember her, and his Aunt Mary had died some years before his father. Of his Aunt Rosamund he knew nothing but believed she was living somewhere in the wilds of Canada. He was glad that the house should go to an old friend of the family as he felt sure this would have pleased his father and aunts.

So that is that, thought Letty. She was not sure whether she was glad or sorry that she was to know so little about those unreal characters — the Lotus House children grown up. She had had some qualms about whether she ought to have mentioned the discovery of the doll's house, but now she decided she could count it in with "the articles contained within the house and the garden at the time of the sale". Six months later, after having disposed of her Bournemouth house satisfactorily, old Mrs Sanderson moved herself into the ground-floor flat of the Lotus House and set about looking for tenants.

CHAPTER THREE

MRS SANDERSON DID not admit to herself that she was influenced in Mrs Royce's favour by the colour of her hair, which was of that warm auburn hue that she had admired above all others ever since she had fallen in love with Rosamund long ago. Nor indeed was it necessary, for there was much else to be said in favour of this, her earliest applicant for the first floor flat. She had a charming smile, was beautifully dressed and was suitably enthusiastic about the whole house.

"I'm always very sensitive to houses, Mrs Sanderson," said Margot Royce, "and yours has such character. You're an answer to prayer, you know. I've been feeling I simply couldn't stand our poky little cottage any longer and this is perfect — two good living-rooms, one quite big enough to take Andrew's piano, it's only a baby grand but it's crowded out our present sitting-room. I must warn you he plays on it quite a lot, I do hope you don't object."

"No," said Letty, hoping the other tenants, when they had materialized, would not do so either, but the walls and ceilings were pretty soundproof, not like modern houses, and anyway, nowadays people were so used to background music of all kinds. So she added that she was fond of music, though she was afraid she did not know much about it.

"Just the same with me," said Margot Royce, "and

three bedrooms too, it will be such a comfort to have a spare room, we've had to put up our guests in our sitting-room, such a bore, and the little room at the end of the passage will do nicely for my small daughter. You don't mind children, do you, Mrs Sanderson? Harriet is a very harmless one."

Mrs Sanderson was really pleased at this. She very much wanted children at the Lotus House again, in fact it turned the scales decisively in Mrs Royce's favour, but she felt a little doubtful about the room at the end of the passage. It had been used as a box-room in the old days, though it did possess a tiny window. Letty could not help thinking it was a pity not to allot one of the proper bedrooms to Harriet, but of course it was not her business.

"It's all just what I might have dreamed of, but never thought to find, and to discover you, too, Mrs Sanderson," said Margot, turning to Letty with that entrancing smile and opening her large very blue eyes wide — "you too, how lucky we shall be to have *you* as our landlady and friend." She drew a silvery scarf round her neck, which was of just the right proportions, not too long and thin, nor too short, like Letty's own. Her thick little neck and, worse still, her double chin, had always been a grief to her. "I must fly," said Margot, "Andrew comes home for lunch and I always like to have something ready for him, and I'm simply longing to tell him all about you and this wonderful flat. We shall certainly want to take it and to move in as soon as possible."

She swept gracefully out of the house and into her rather shabby little Mini, leant forward to wave through the window and was off, leaving Letty, quite delighted, on the doorstep.

"I don't think I could do better," she said to herself contentedly, and it was only later that she remembered that she had not said anything about references.

"One thing I must impress upon you, my dear Mrs Sanderson," Mr Donovan had said, "don't agree to anything without taking up references, and be sure you don't trust to written ones only; I will gladly investigate personally myself if you would like me to do so."

So kind of him, thought Letty, *and now I have practically agreed to let the best flat without even mentioning the matter. Still, I'm sure it's all right. He is a Doctor of Science, she said, and she is so delightful, such lovely hair and obviously a good wife too, and with a little girl nearly eight years old.* She confessed her lapse to Mr Donovan but there was such a gleam in her eye as she did so that, though he intended to look into the matter himself, he was convinced that nothing less than a proven record for crime could shake her determination to allow Dr and Mrs Royce and Harriet to move in as soon as possible.

If she had slipped up over references for the Royces, Mrs Sanderson was able to produce impeccable ones for Aubrey Stacey, the would-be tenant of the top-floor flat. He was a schoolmaster, a bachelor with a brother who was a barrister. Moreover he and his brother had both been educated at Westminster. *Such a coincidence*, thought Letty with pleasure, for Westminster had been Edward's public school. She remembered this because he had once impressed her with its superiority over all other public schools. "It is the only one left up in London, the only one that counts, and London is the greatest city in the world." Yes, of course, he had told her this at George V's coronation. Edward had been in the upper school then and had a seat in the Abbey with the Westminster boys. This proved his point. Of course this had been long before Aubrey Stacey's time. He had read English at Oxford and was on the staff of a neighbouring large comprehensive school. He was not very communicative about his career but she got the impression that besides teaching he also wrote a little.

"Aubrey Stacey, an attractive name, don't you think? And he looks like Shelley," Letty said to Mr Donovan. "At least," she added honestly, "he has a brow like Shelley's." His receding chin beneath a straggling beard were less impressive, but he was an old Westminster boy with a poetic forehead and had a barrister for a brother.

"I don't consider that Shelley would have been a very desirable tenant," said Mr Donovan. Really, there was no satisfying him! "Still," he admitted, "he is certainly respectably connected. I think I have heard of that brother of his and he has a secure job."

Letty discovered another point in Mr Stacey's favour — he seemed to take especially to the old night nursery. No one had happened to tell the workmen to remove the bars from the windows and Letty apologized for this.

"I remember peering through such bars with my brother," he said smiling. "We used to play that we were monkeys in the zoo. I think I should like them left, so don't trouble about them. I shall make this my bedroom, Mrs Sanderson, if I am lucky enough to be allowed to take your attractive flat. It is on the quiet side of the house and I am a poor sleeper."

"Do you know," said Letty, "I often used to sleep here myself as a child and I remember the shadow of those very same bars falling across the whole room in a pattern. You'll think me fanciful, I expect, but I still feel this room is the safest place in all the world."

The basement flat took the longest to be settled for there were several applicants before a really satisfactory one materialized. There was the young couple, unmarried, uninhibited and very untidy. Old Mrs Sanderson was not yet acclimatized to the permissive society and although she found the couple interesting, she was bewildered by them. The girl announced that she was an artist, "entirely committed". What the young man did she never

31

discovered — he remained speechless throughout the interview. "We want to find somewhere to leave our things while we tramp around Europe for the next month or so," explained the girl. "You see, I am not sure yet whether Jason is quite sound on the baroque and it makes a difference to our future. I may not wish to remain with him, but in any case if we take the flat, it will be in my name and I shall be responsible." But to Letty this did not appear a promising enough proposition for the Lotus House, whatever Jason might think of the baroque.

Then there was the anxious lady with the cats. Not that she was physically accompanied by them but they were very much with her in spirit.

"I am having to give up my home, alas, since my friend with whom I have shared it hitherto has moved away. There was a little difference between us about the pussies. It is quite a large house and what with the rates and the repairs and the heating, I cannot keep it on alone and must find somewhere smaller. But the pussies — I had ten of them and I've managed to find homes for Don and Titus and Sammy and Bogey. It's the girls who are the problem, though they are not really so, the dears, they are so good and I should hate to lose any of them. Susie is a wonderful mother and Di, she's the huntress, why she even caught a swallow once, and Plush is so affectionate, and of course it's out of the question to part with Clytemnestra, the largest black Persian that ever was seen I assure you, Mrs Sanderson, and Yum Yum and Peep Bo are Siamese and were given me by a dear, dear friend. So you see I must have a flat with an access to a nice garden and this would suit me perfectly. You've no idea how hard it has been to find just the right place for my little family."

Letty felt she did indeed know just how hard it had been and was still going to be, for she wondered how long the nice garden would remain nice with six cats dividing it between them — and would they even stay at six with

32

Susie being such a good mother? Besides, she loved birds as well as flowers, so she screwed up her courage to say "No" and to send the poor cat lady reproachfully and sorrowfully on her way.

At last, after one or two more unsatisfactory aspirants, a Miss Cook arrived from the agents one day. She was a retired Post Office official. Letty gathered that she had inherited a little money lately and wanted to settle in a place of her own.

"My brother is selling my parents' house with my full consent. I think I would prefer a flat if it is entirely self-contained."

"Oh yes," said Letty, "this is the most self-contained flat in the whole house because it is the only one with a separate entrance, as you see."

The basement, having practically no associations with the child Letty, and needing more radical conversion than any other part of the building, had been turned over to the architect without restrictions. As a result it was the most convenient of the flats with really modern offices, all shining with tiles and white paint and stainless steel. The big old kitchen had been divided into a very pleasant small sitting-room and a bedroom — the sitting-room with a door opening into the garden.

Miss Cook had a singularly inexpressive countenance. Her black hair was cut close in a tight fringed cap. She had the type of face that one cannot imagine as ever having looked young. It had a small buttoned-up mouth and round black eyes, and her cheeks, innocent of face powder, were reddened with a network of roughened veins. Letty wondered why she looked vaguely familiar. Later it suddenly came to her — Miss Cook reminded her of a Dutch doll — indeed of one particular Dutch doll, the one that had been Mr and Mrs Golightly's cook in Selina's doll's house, and who had been selected at the toy shop for this purpose because of Jane, the cook, in

33

Beatrix Potter's *Two Bad Mice*, but Selina had not called her Jane, she had always just been 'Cooksie'.

"Of course," Letty said to herself, very amused at the thought, "the resemblance is striking and her name actually *is* Cook. How very right and proper to have a cook in the basement of the Lotus House again, only unfortunately she's not a real one. How convenient if she were." She had yet to cope with the problem of domestic help for herself — the lodgers would see to their own rooms, of course, but she felt she herself would like some help if she could get it.

Miss Cook, or 'Cooksie' as Letty could not help secretly calling her, provided a watertight reference from the Post Office and was accepted for the basement flat, and so the problem of tenants was settled to Mrs Sanderson's satisfaction.

Meanwhile they in their turn were summing up their future landlady and the Lotus House. Margot Royce, as she drove away, not actually to prepare a meal for a husband but to keep an appointment with her hairdresser, congratulated herself on a good morning's work. She had left a note for Andrew about his lunch, she herself would have a sandwich and a cup of coffee while her hair was being re-tinted. She got back to the cottage a couple of hours later to find, as she expected, that he had not bothered with eating, but was busy working out some problem in his head while playing accurately and endlessly one of Bach's Fugues.

"I think it will do very nicely," she said switching on the cooker.

"What will?" enquired Andrew politely at the end of the next bar.

"That flat I told you I was going to see this morning, nice rooms, good outlook, good garage and convenient for shops."

"Good," said Andrew again, and then, more attentive-

34

ly, "you sound like a house agent. What about the rent?" Though he admitted that Margot had quite a flair for business, yet she was apt to be oblivious of costs once she had set her heart on something.

She named the rent and Andrew lifted his eyebrows. "You can't get anything decent for much less in that neighbourhood, really, Andrew."

"We can't afford that *and* Harriet's school," he said.

"Oh well," said Margot, "she'll have to leave, then. Anyway it's about time she got away from Queensmead now, she's had long enough there."

"You said the other day she was so happy that it would be a mistake to move her for another year at least."

"It wasn't the other day, it was last term. Mrs Campbell's over-protective, I consider, and it's time Harriet learned to rough it a bit at an ordinary school. There's a good one within easy reach I believe — I'll make enquiries."

Andrew said no more. He did not particularly want to move from the cottage, but he was not unprepared. He had noticed apprehensively when it had turned from being "an adorable find, so easy to heat and look at the garden, a dream, and really plenty of room for your piano," into "a poky little hole with your piano taking up the whole sitting-room, and the garden! Neither of us have time to cope with it, it's absurd."

Before the cottage there had been the seaside maisonette: "so good for all our healths, the air like wine and a marvellous train service . . . " but this in its turn had become "too inaccessible and really a little vulgar, don't you think?"

The frequent moves were expensive but Andrew's motto was "anything for a quiet life".

"At last there will be plenty of room for your piano and it's nearer both our jobs."

"Good," said Andrew for the third time. He had slight

qualms about Harriet, but she was not his child and therefore not his responsibility, he told himself.

"Mrs Sanderson said she wouldn't mind how much you played."

"Who's Mrs Sanderson?"

"Our prospective landlady."

"What's she like?" asked Andrew without much interest.

"Oh, I don't know, just ordinary I think, the kind of person who adores Betjeman's poetry and goes to the Academy and shops at Marks & Sparks. Well, I'm not sure about the last. She's got some really good rugs in her room, though not much else. She's rather sweet really and likes children. She'll be good for some baby-sitting I should think when we want an evening out."

"I should think so too," said Andrew, "if you want it that way she hasn't much choice."

"Eat your lunch," said Margot, "it's disgracefully late."

Aubrey Stacey walked away from the Lotus House across the heath with a sense of relief which was the nearest thing he got to happiness nowadays. The flat had an atmosphere of peace about it — that old nursery with the bars had taken him right back in time to his own nursery days which he had shared with his twin, his boon playmate and companion, before the years had separated them. The view towards London was transformed by the autumn mist into an ethereal and lovely city. Even the highrise flats and offices looked like fairytale towers. Aubrey, always sensitive to beauty, felt his heart lightened and the hope sprang up that this move would prove a fresh start for him. At the other side of the heath he boarded a bus which landed him near his present noisy lodgings, a shabby house shared with three other members of the school staff. How glad he would be to be free of them, and they, too, of him, he conceded wryly. What

36

a mistake it always was to live with colleagues. He ardently hoped that Mrs Sanderson would not go back on her word, but the old school tie seemed to have done the trick. It was lucky that Westminster had happened to crop up in the conversation and that she had had some connection with the place.

Miss Cook was also pleased with the Lotus House. That kitchen and that bathroom — really nice they were! Of course, everything needed a good clean up, one could see that, in spite of the workmen pretending they'd done it already, and the rooms would look much better still when she'd finished with them. The sitting-room got a bit too much sun for her covers and carpet, but she would get some really substantial curtains to keep it off. Of course there would be drawbacks, there always were to everything. Still, Mrs Sanderson seemed a pleasant sort of person; a bit untidy-looking and the front hall and stairs might have looked cleaner there was no denying, but these wouldn't be her province. She had her own entrance, that was really a good point; her's was much the most private of all the flats, and she needn't meet the other tenants at all really unless she wished, and she couldn't see herself wishing it. She thought her furniture would all fit in well. She'd see about those curtains as soon as possible.

Everyone was settled in before Christmas and Letty Sanderson woke one morning in her new bedroom which had been the old dining-room and felt the house once again full of life around her. She sighed with satisfaction. She was getting used to sleeping in her august surroundings, for the room still kept for her something of its original dignity. It had been the most formal in the house, but she had replaced the dark red paper of her memories with a pale grey distemper and the heavy red curtains by striped blue and green linen. She lay and looked up at the ceiling, admiring its graceful mouldings which she had certainly never noticed as a child. They were too far away she supposed or, more probably, she had always been too pleasantly busy to spend time staring upwards. In one corner of the room the doll's house now stood on a special stand she had had made for it. She looked forward to showing it to Harriet who, she thought with satisfaction, must soon be home for the Christmas holidays.

She heard a thump on the floor above, the opening and shutting of doors and later someone running down the stairs. She wondered if that was Mr Stacey or Dr Royce. Then a happy idea occurred to her. She would give a party at Christmas so that everyone could meet each other properly. It would be a party for the Lotus House too, to celebrate its starting to become a home once more, for she cherished the dream that they all might settle down so comfortably together that they would form a really happy, friendly community. It would be repaying a sort of debt to the past.

CHAPTER FOUR

WHILE MRS SANDERSON, in her bedroom on the first floor, was lying at ease planning her party, Miss Cook in the basement was sitting down to a well-earned cup of coffee and piece of toast after a good hour's work at further unpacking and cleaning and tidying up. She felt tired but appeased. It really did begin to look nice, she thought. She had carried her tray from the kitchen into the sitting-room where the wintry sun was just beginning to send slanting rays through her new curtains. "In summer I shall have to draw them," she said to herself, "can't have my new covers fading — they say these new materials are guaranteed, but you can't trust them, that's the worst of a south-facing room and the carpet, it can't afford to look worse than it does now, either." She gave it a resentful little kick.

She would have loved to have got everything new, she would have kept her grandfather's chair, of course, and her mother's best china, but that was all. She had been left the furniture and quite right too, but Henry would have been welcome to it if she could have afforded to replace it. Oh well, it had fitted in quite well here — the glass-fronted cupboard, you couldn't see a smear on it now and the china showed up well inside. She was glad she'd had grandfather's chair re-covered, pricey though it was. It looked handsome now, nobody could say it didn't, and the curtains were pretty though, looking at them from where she sat, she thought they could have done with a bit more length to them. This worried her, had she spoiled the ship for a ha'p'orth of tar? But she was really glad she had chosen that colour — she'd always favoured pink. Henry's Doris had wanted her to have green, quite cross she'd been about it, always had to be right, had Doris, came of being a schoolmistress she supposed. "There's plenty of green outside," she'd said to her — it was different at home with nothing but pavements and houses, but here there would be always something green to look at, even in winter. She could see some sort of evergreen bush now in a corner over by the fence. She had been told that the strip of garden below her windows belonged to her. "Well, I don't know that I want it," she had said to Mrs 'Sanderson. "I've never had anything to do with gardening." But on thinking it over she rather liked the idea, she could learn, she supposed. *Better than having someone else poking about so close any old time*, she thought. They hadn't had a garden at home, just a square of coloured pavement in front and a yard at the back for dustbins and washing. The house was in one of those utterly characterless suburbs of London, a district which was neither going up nor down. Its streets gave away nothing about their inhabitants — far less than did the neighbouring large cemetery about its graves.

No doubt Albert Street, where Miss Cook's home had been, contained some happy lively families but the Cooks' was not one of these. The dominating factor in all their lives was that Mrs Cook had married beneath her. Her father had been a country clergyman, without any private income and therefore of straitened means, but undeniably, by reason of his profession, a gentleman. She had been romantically inclined towards a young Air Force flight sub-lieutenant quartered in a nearby camp during the latter part of the first world war. But after the marriage, and Armistice Day when the uniform was laid by, there was found to have been nothing much inside it. Untrained for any civilian post and without influence and not very intelligent, Sydney Cook had failed in one job after another and had ended up driving a laundry van. Disappointed and resentful, his wife had concentrated on bringing up her two children — Henry, named for her father and Janet for her mother. She taught them to keep themselves to themselves and to despise their father. The neighbours in Albert Street where they were forced to live were potentially threatening to Mrs Cook's self-respect and her son and daughter were strictly forbidden to play with the other children in the street. She starved her family of all indulgences so that she might send Henry and Janet to second-rate private schools where they made no real friends — the right sort in Mrs Cook's eyes could not well be asked home, and the wrong sort were frowned upon. On the whole both children, she considered, had justified the care bestowed on them. They each qualified for respectable white-collar jobs and their mother died happy in the thought that she could now meet her Maker and her father (she had never really distinguished between them) with a clear conscience. By then Henry had made an entirely suitable marriage — his Doris was a schoolteacher and kept on her job. Janet had tried nursing but had found the paper-work difficult and had also had trouble with her back, so had given it up and entered the ranks of the Civil Service instead. She had qualified as a Post Office assistant. As for their father, he had driven his van and brought back his wages and eaten his meals, and bestowed a few furtive caresses on Janet when she was little, and gradually became invisible, and one day he had a stroke and died. His daughter could scarcely recall either his face or his voice. The voice of her mother, on the other hand, she remembered very well as an ever-admonishing wail — "do this, do that", or

41

more often, "don't do this, don't do that". When she actually heard it no more in the flesh, she felt at first stunned by the silence and even yet, especially whenever she sat down to rest, as she was doing at this moment, sipping her coffee and warming her toes by her now gleaming electric fire, she heard it echoing in her mind and felt it unwise to be too pleased with her new quarters.

"There's sure to be snags," she reminded herself, almost with a sense of satisfaction. There were the other lodgers, for instance, "not nosey, that's all I ask," and she congratulated herself once again on having a separate entrance. "You can't be too careful."

The sounds of departure Mrs Sanderson had heard that morning were neither Andrew Royce nor Aubrey Stacey, but Margot setting out for her art gallery. Physics research laboratories keeping later hours, Andrew was still finishing a leisurely breakfast. The move had been accomplished with Margot's usual efficiency and though he did not care for these upheavals, he had to admit that each was managed with as little inconvenience to himself as possible. All that was left to him was the unpacking and arranging of his books, music and records and there was certainly more room for these here than there had been in the cottage. It was always a source of amused wonder to him that anyone so pretty and feminine as Margot could be so businesslike, but he did not think about this for long. People did not interest him very much. An only child, his relationship with his parents was amiable but distant. They were both always very occupied — his father as a GP and his mother as a practising physiotherapist. A capable nanny, prep school from the age of seven, followed by his public school, Cambridge and a year in the United States had not provided much opportunity for cultivating home ties.

At school he was sufficiently good at games to be allowed to go his own way without interference and this way was that of a natural loner, increasingly absorbed in music and science. At college these had continued his main interests, and self-sufficiency had grown to be a habit. He had not mixed much with women but when he happened to meet Margot, older and more experienced than himself, he quickly fell under her spell. He had never seen anyone who charmed his senses so completely. They neither of them wanted marriage. She had fairly recently broken up a first unsatisfactory one, and was firmly set against a second, and Andrew was unwilling to undertake any definite commitment that might threaten his work in any possible direction. He was not unduly worried when he learned of the existence of Harriet.

"She's at a home school at present," said Margot, "I promise you she won't be a nuisance."

"That's all right," said Andrew. He knew very little about children and anyway it was Margot who mattered. He discovered quite soon that she was untruthful, self-centred, a snob and amazingly restless, but none of this troubled him overmuch. He had always accepted people as he found them with the same detached lucidity that he brought to his work. Physically, she enchanted him — it was like living with a rose. He sometimes wondered how long this state of affairs would last, but in spite of Margot's love of change, it seemed to have become a habit with both of them.

As for Harriet, he found somewhat to his surprise that he quite liked having her about. She reminded him of a small mongrel dog he had had as a boy and been very fond of, but he was glad that she was unlike the dog in that she showed no special liking for himself, which would have bothered him, but it was obvious even to the unobservant Andrew that she had no devotion to spare for anyone but her mother. This was unfortunate for Margot was not cut out for motherhood. He wondered why she had ever had a child — he could not suppose her husband had wanted it, he had shown absolutely no interest in Harriet as far as Andrew knew since the marriage had broken up, and besides, he did not think that Dick's wishes would rank very high as a factor in the case. He supposed it was consistent with her inclination to try everything once. These ruminations of his were aroused by Margot's decision not to bring Harriet home for Christmas. "We shan't be settled in properly before all the rush is over and it'll simply be a nuisance having her around. I'll fetch her in plenty of time for the new school term," she had said.

Margot herself considered Harriet her second big mistake, worse of course because the child was lacking in attraction, which she could not have foreseen. Still, it had been foolish to risk so much merely because she hoped that a baby would bring her the sort of fulfilment that it was said to supply to most women. The first mistake was, of course, her marriage, which she rushed into to escape from a home which was simply a wearisome battlefield.

Her father came from humble origins but possessed a good business head and had raised himself to the position of land agent on a large estate in the West Country — "my father's place in Dorset" as Margot was wont to refer casually to it. He had married a town-bred wife whom he had admired for her delicate prettiness, but this soon withered from boredom and indulgence, and she had developed a waspish neurotic temperament. They kept together, Margot supposed on looking back, partly because divorce then was both more difficult and more expensive — her father was always mean about money — and partly because mutual dislike seemed to have habituated them to a habit of scoring off each other, which brought a certain spice into their relationship. Their daughter became a pawn in these unpleasant games. Her looks and her intelligence made her a valuable asset as a possession. Incessant forays took place over her education, clothes, friends, almost every possible debatable point. Her father, who held the purse strings, generally came off as the victor, but her mother scored points by running up large housekeeping and dress bills and by occasionally staging a bout of frightening hysteria. Margot learned from an early age to play off one parent against another and that, both from them and from most other people, she could get what she wanted by the exercise of her beguiling charm. But then, what did she want? Certainly not Dick Harper after the first year, nor motherhood apparently. Lovers? Too easy to subjugate and too tiresome when enslaved. Success in her business? Yes, because she despised failures, but somehow this wasn't enough. Meanwhile there was Andrew whose demands were so simple, whose detachment intrigued her, and whose brains commanded her respect.

Aubrey Stacey was busy hanging pictures. Over the fireplace in the room which had been the old night nursery, he hung a college group. He had gone up to Oxford because his twin brother had been a Trinity scholar at Cambridge, where he had taken a double first. Almost as soon as they outgrew their babyhood, Aubrey had realized that he was fated to play second fiddle to Michael — if indeed he counted at all in his mother's eyes. "Is that you, darling?" he heard her cry sometimes when he had come home from school and he knew enough to answer: "No, it's me, Mother."

His father, on the other hand, had always been painfully determined to play fair. "It's rough luck on the boy," he would say to his friends, "that Michael happens to be rather a brilliant fellow all-round, though I say it myself. Aubrey should have been a girl, he'd have made a good one — he'd not have felt the competition then and it would have been natural the way his mother feels — mothers and sons, you know, and I would have liked a daughter myself too, but we've got to take what comes haven't we, till the scientist chaps have changed all that for us. Anyway, Aubrey will make it, I always say."

What "making it" meant exactly had never been quite clear. A minor exhibition in English to one of the less distinguished colleges at Oxford, a respectable second-class degree, one need not be ashamed of these, but they were perhaps not exactly "making it". Nonetheless, he had been happier at Oxford than at any other period of his life. He had been adopted by a set aspiring to the creative arts, had contributed several poems to a university magazine and had initiated a private resolve to "make it" in an entirely different but unmistakably as equally a successful manner as his brother, by writing a magnum opus. After much heart-searching he had decided on a subject. Actually this had been suggested to him by a sympathetic tutor — "I had thought of working him up myself one day but I don't suppose I shall ever get down to it, so I make you a present of him, Stacey."

The "him" in question was the 17th century bibliophile Sir Robert Cotton, who had devoted his life to collecting books, but who, in 1629, had been accused of sedition and whose beloved library was taken from him, which had broken his heart. The tutor had envisaged a scholarly monograph, but Aubrey was after fame and as wide a public as possible. He thought in terms of an historical novel — of a high literary standard, of course, serious in intent, with leanings towards mysticism and tragedy. Sitting in the Bodleian, whose founder, Sir Thomas Bodley, had been Cotton's friend, it was easy to envisage such a splendid achievement, but after he had gone down from Oxford the initial impulse had waned a little. Still, a sizeable pile of manuscript now lay in a drawer of the bureau which was his most prized piece of furniture, a present from his brother, who had always treated him with the greatest affection and generosity and for whom he felt a blend of devotion and envy but never of resentment — *that* he kept for his parents.

A great literary work in the making could not support him so he had taken a teacher-training course and then a post as English master in a small sedate grammar school, where he had spent two uneventful years until it had been swallowed up by the neighbouring comprehensive. From that time on his troubles had begun. It was a completely different world demanding a robust self-confidence and the gift of establishing an easy relationship with the young. Aubrey possessed neither. Most of his pupils now came from a different background than his own, and he felt them alien to him, especially the girls, with their nonchalance and flaunting jokes and latent contempt, which grew in proportion to his own nervousness and inadequacy with them. Certain classes took on a nightmarish quality. He turned to his great work for comfort, but it was easier to plan it and to dream of it rather than to get down to the actual writing. He told himself that he must allow it to well up from his inner being — the sub-conscious, where all works of genius were conceived. But increasingly he seemed to need a stimulus to switch on: a glass or two of alcohol helped considerably. Now however, with this move, he hoped somehow that everything would take a turn for the better.

It was from this material that the innocent old Mrs Sanderson hoped to fashion a happy family group. There was indeed a common link between them, but this happened to be that none of them had experienced what it really meant to be a member of a family at all.

Letty was disappointed to learn that Harriet was not coming to the Lotus House for Christmas. She had planned her party to contain a Christmas tree with a child in mind. She could not help wondering at that delightful Mrs Royce apparently not longing for her little daughter to come home at once, as soon as the flat was habitable, especially for Christmas. Margot sensed this slight disapproval and reacted to it immediately.

"You see, Mrs Sanderson, Harriet has all her little friends at Queensmead, which isn't at all like an ordinary school, and they have a perfectly splendid time at Christmas, much better than she could have here, except for your lovely party, of course." She also managed delicately to hint that it was Andrew who was not too anxious for Harriet's company. It was now for the first time that Letty learned that Harriet was the child of a former marriage, though Margot did not think it necessary to divulge the fact that she was not legally Mrs Royce at all. She always found it better to adapt facts to her audience.

"Andrew is terribly good with her, of course, but he doesn't like to be put out in the way children can't help doing; you know what men are!"

Letty went away thinking that of course as Harriet was not Dr Royce's child, it must make it difficult sometimes for poor Mrs Royce. She had not taken to Andrew much, a bit superior and standoffish, she thought him. She decided to have the tree all the same. She felt sure that there had always been a Christmas tree at the Lotus House in the old days, though she had never been privileged to see it, and she was determined that the house should have its tree once more, and that it should have real candles on it and not the dead garish brilliance of those horrid coloured electric bulbs. It took her a long while to track down clip-on holders for the candles, but she found some at last. She also bought crackers and presents and ordered a special Christmas cake from the Honey Pot who were doing the catering for her. The cake was to have "Welcome to the Lotus House" written on it in silver balls. "Everyone is a child at heart at Christmas," Letty told herself delusively. She had worked hard and while she sat awaiting her guests, she looked round with satisfied delight. The room, she thought, looked charming — a well-shaped tree all ready to be lit up, her father's silver branched candlesticks on either side of the cake in the centre of the table which was decorated with the prettiest candles she had been able to find, a bowl of white chrysanthemums and scarlet-berried holly on the mantelpiece above the lively fragrant log fire and a fine piece of mistletoe suspended above the door. Everything, like herself, was waiting expectantly for the curtain to go up and the fun to begin.

There is nothing quite so flat and dreary as a party that never takes off and it is even more distressing when this happens at times that demand a specially festive spirit.

"Laugh, damn you, laugh," swore Mr Donovan inwardly, as the guests pulled their crackers and donned their paper hats almost in silence. He had just read out one of those sublimely silly cracker jokes, but it had perished in mid-air.

Mr Donovan had been invited to the party by his old client and had come purely out of the kindness of his heart, but he did not like parties. That was the trouble, they none of them did. Aubrey and Andrew thought them a tiresome waste of time, Miss Cook distrusted them because her mother had, especially the parties in Albert Street. "You never know who you might meet there," she used to say. Of course Miss Cook did know who she was going to meet at this particular party, but she did not particularly want to meet any of them. In Margot's eyes this boring childish gathering hardly qualified as a party at all. Nonetheless, she could not help saving it from total failure. She sparkled at Mr Donovan, admired Miss Cook's unbecoming dress and to Letty she cried, "Mrs Sanderson, you're a magician, I haven't seen a tree with candles since Christmas at my old country home, my father's place in Dorset, where *did* you find them?"

The candles, indeed, provided the only real glory of Letty's party, and as she extinguished them she acknowledged ruefully that it certainly had not achieved its

49

purpose. The mistletoe mocked her. "How stupid of me to put it up." The scarcely-touched cake reproached her. "Nobody really wanted me," it seemed to say, and indeed no one but Andrew had eaten much of the lavish meal. He had set about it with his usual whole-hearted concentration on the business in hand.

"How you could eat at that ungodly hour I can't imagine," said Margot (the party had been fixed early to suit Mr Donovan, who did not wish to be late home). She tossed the embroidered linen handkerchiefs that Letty had chosen for her into her "bring and buy" drawer — she never used anything but tissues. Miss Cook was taking one of her digestive pills which she usually did as a precaution after a meal out, and eyeing with malevolence the gorgeous bottle of bath salts which she had received. "I am *sure* she never buys herself little luxuries," Letty had thought, "it's expensive but Cooksie shall have a treat for once." But Janet Cook had never used bath salts in her life and never meant to. "Just waste, stinks the place out and muddies up nice clear water." Whatever was she to do with it? She might give it to Henry's Doris, only as she never gave her presents like that, it would seem queer, it was a real worry!

"A party in a parlour, all silent and all damned," quoted Aubrey Stacey to himself as he thankfully ran up the stairs to his attic fastness.

But old Mrs Sanderson firmly put away disheartening thoughts together with all the remains of the food, the candle-holders and the present-wrappings. She must not be in a hurry, she told herself, it was early days yet, give them time and they would all be friends, she felt sure. Meanwhile there was Harriet's arrival to look forward to.

CHAPTER FIVE

HARRIET WAS USED to changes; she did not much like them, though. She did not really want to leave Queensmead because she had been at school there since she was five and a half and she was now nearly eight, and that was a long time. She had almost got a best friend now, too. When you were little, it didn't matter not having one so much, but later it began to matter. The friend had not been at Queensmead very long, and she had been glad of Harriet because she had a squint and they called her 'Squinty' — her real name was Mandy. They called Harriet 'Fatty', not being very inventive at Queensmead, and the two got left out of things together which was better than being left out of them alone, though Harriet secretly didn't like Squinty all that much.

But Margot arrived after Christmas was over and told her that she was to go to a more grown-up school. This was frightening but exciting and, what was more important even, she was to live at home with Margot and Andrew and go every day to this school from a new house. Margot had told Harriet to call them Margot and Andrew when she was six. She had never called Andrew "Daddy" anyway because he wasn't her real father, so she hadn't called him anything, and secretly she still called Margot "Mummy" to herself. She thought her the most beautiful and wonderful mother that anyone could have.

She knew the other children at Queensmead thought so too. When Margot came to visit Harriet she talked to them all and Harriet could see them liking it because she was so pretty and wore such lovely clothes. This was Harriet's one claim to fame, but though she gloried in her mother, she had also felt sorry and ashamed for some time now, ever since one of the children had said to her "You're not a bit like your mother, are you?" Once she had firmly believed she would grow like her when she was older, then she hoped desperately that she might — "O God, let me be, O God, let me be!" — but now she knew she wouldn't ever be. She felt it deep down inside.

When her mother came to Queensmead this time and explained that Harriet was to leave, she brought a big box of chocolates for her to give to all her friends and though, except for Squinty, she knew they weren't really her friends, she enjoyed handing them round and hearing everyone say how lucky she was to be going away from horrid old school with such a lovely mother. Mrs Campbell, the headmistress, was sorry to lose Harriet who was a quiet, if unresponsive, child and gave little trouble, unlike some of her other charges for whom Queensmead was a substitute home "especially designed to meet the needs of those children whose parents were, for reasons of all sorts, unable to provide a home for themselves".

"I can't thank you enough, Mrs Campbell, for all you have done for Harriet," said Margot and her upward gaze, for Mrs Campbell was tall and thin, was so expressive of deep gratitude that Mrs Campbell thought that she must somehow have had more effect on the child than she had supposed.

As they drove away Harriet's mild feeling of regret at leaving and her anxiety as to the future were temporarily swamped by delight as she realized that this was one of Margot's good times. Except for one complaint that she grew out of her clothes faster than anyone would think possible, there seemed nothing wrong with her at present, and Margot had called her "darling" twice — once in front of Mrs Campbell, which hardly counted, but once when they were alone together and when they stopped halfway for refreshment, she was allowed to have a chocolate éclair. "It won't matter for once," said Margot, looking at the stout square child opposite her with resignation. *Really, she grows more like Dick every day*, she thought.

Harriet was very pleased to hear that she was going to have a bedroom of her own in the new house. This had never happened to her before as long as she could remember. At school she had slept with Lucy and Rebecca who had secrets and ignored her and, at the cottage, when she was there which wasn't very often, she slept on a folding-bed in a sort of alcove between the bathroom and Andrew's room.

"Has it got a window?" she enquired anxiously. A bedroom wasn't a proper one with no window, and she had always wanted to be able to lie in bed and look out of one. Lucy and Rebecca could do this but she had had to look at a blank wall.

"Yes, of course," said Margot.

When they got to the Lotus House it was getting dark and Harriet was tired. Being with Margot was marvellous but it always made her feel as if she had run a long way rather fast, as if there was a clock ticking inside her that wouldn't stop.

"Don't leave me to carry all the things in," said Margot, "you're quite old enough now to try and be helpful. You can manage that case — why, your arms are almost as long and big as mine."

Harriet picked up the case, she knew her arms ought not to be so long and big at her age. She followed her mother into the hall, blinking at the bright light. An old lady came bustling out of a door to greet them.

"Well, here we are, Mrs Sanderson," said her mother, "all safe and sound, and this is my little Harriet. Harriet, this is our very kind landlady. She's been longing to meet you. Say 'How do you do', Harriet." But Harriet, who had not until this moment heard anything of Mrs Sanderson, just stared, and Mrs Sanderson's smile of welcome grew a little fixed.

"How could Mrs Royce have produced such a very plain daughter?" she thought and then, feeling at once remorseful for such an idea, she bent down and kissed her. She felt Harriet stiffen and said to herself, "This child isn't used to being kissed."

If Mrs Sanderson was disappointed at her first sight of Harriet, Harriet was as disappointed in her bedroom. It was hardly bigger than the cottage alcove.

"It *hasn't* got a window," she said crossly, "Margot said it had." Margot had gone straight to her own room and it didn't matter what she said to Andrew.

"Yes, it has," said Andrew, "look, the roof slopes out here and it is just above the bed." Harriet looked up and saw a small square of glass that opened with a pulley.

"But you can't see out of it," she said.

Andrew switched off the light. "Now look," he said. In the frosty January sky the stars were brilliant.

"You are the only person who can lie in bed and see the sky properly," said Andrew, "and it's always changing." He switched on the light again.

"The bathroom's along there next to my room — you'd better have a wash and then supper will be ready. I bet you're hungry."

Left alone, Harriet switched off the light once more and gazed up at the stars. She thought she had never really seen them before. Her room was a proper bedroom after all, and it was the only one in which you could lie in your bed and see the sky above you. Andrew had said so.

"Hurry up, Harriet," came Margot's voice down the passage, "supper's ready," and Harriet hurried.

The next few days were a rush of getting ready for the new school. A uniform had to be bought. Harriet had looked forward to this, it seemed grand and important for there had been no school uniform at Queensmead.

"I'm afraid she's at least two sizes larger than the average for her age," said Margot, smiling apologetically at the young shop assistant. "It's a quite hideous brown, don't you think?" she went on, "Why, do you suppose, any school should want to choose anything so unbecoming? *You* could carry it off with that nice fair colouring, but for anyone sallow it's abominable."

Harriet, listening, knew without any doubt from the way the shop assistant then looked at her that she must be the "anyone sallow". "Sallow", she hadn't met the word before and it sounded horrid. The day's shopping with her mother to which she had eagerly looked forward became as dust and ashes.

"Really, dragging that child about London got me down," complained Margot that night.

"What does sallow mean?" Harriet asked Andrew next time they were alone together. You could ask Andrew things safely because he never wanted to know why you asked them.

"Sallow," he said, not bothering to look up from the paper he was reading, "it either means a kind of willow-tree or a sort of greyish, yellow colour - rather a nasty colour really." That was that then. She knew she wasn't a tree so she must have a sort of greyish yellow face. Perhaps that was the reason she hadn't ever had a proper friend — no one would want to have a person of that sort who was also called 'Fatty' for a best friend. She examined her face closely in the bathroom mirror, she hadn't one of her own, and it was true, though she had never noticed it before, her face wasn't pink and white

55

like her mother's or red and brown like Andrew's, it was sallow, sallow, sallow. And soon she would have to take it to the new school in the now hated uniform, but perhaps she would die first. "Oh, God, let me die now." But she didn't die, and at first school was so noisy and crowded and altogether bewildering that she was too stunned to think of anything at all. She was always getting lost in endless passages and bells rang suddenly, which meant you had to be in another classroom, or in the cloakroom, or in the hall, or in the playground, and she was hardly ever in the right place or knew how to get there.

After some time, though, it got easier and there were so many people at this school that they didn't seem to notice her much as long as she kept quiet, and by the second term, though she hadn't found a friend, she *had* found a hero. He was a boy in the same class and he had found her on one of those early days when she had got hopelessly lost, and had told her where she ought to be and had taken her there. He had freckles and a nice grin and hair like a yellow bush, and she had found out that his name was Ben. He could do handstands longer than any one else and keep two balls going up in the air for ages, too, and he actually lived in the housing estate at the back of the Lotus House. After she knew that she used to watch for him, over the fence, hidden in the old lilac bushes. Margot had said the garden didn't really belong to them at all — the bit by the basement flat belonged to Miss Cook and the rest to Mrs Sanderson, who had kindly said that Harriet could play there whenever she wanted to. She didn't want to play there. There was nothing to play at and no one to play with, but she spent quite a long while watching the children playing on the estate. There were two distinct groups of these — one she called "the Terribles" who were mostly the older ones. Harriet did not dare to be seen by any of these. They fought and shouted and threw things about; once they were throwing things at a poor cat, but it escaped, and scrambling over the fence in its desperation, rushed into Miss Cook's part of the garden and then disappeared. The boys continued to throw a few stones after it over the fence — one nearly hit Harriet and so she dared not go in search of the cat until they had all gone away, but she could not find it. Instead Miss Cook found her and was cross with her for "trespassing", as she called it.

Of the other younger group Ben was the leader. Harriet, worshipping from afar, saw with approval that it was he who arranged all the games and that the others did what he told them. He was nearly always the centre of a crowd, but sometimes he would come out later, just before the "Terribles", and practise by himself with a ball. One never-to-be-forgotten day he was there alone when Harriet came out and he actually looked over the fence and hailed her.

"Hullo, kid, I've sent my ball over by mistake. Can I come and look for it?"

Harriet nodded, she was speechless with shyness and emotion. She stood stock still until Ben appeared again on her side of the fence.

"There's an awful lot of long grass and bushes," he said, "I didn't see where it went. Can you help? You look along here and I'll start further off."

Harriet began to look but without hope, her mother always said she could never find anything. And then she saw it, something red, half-hidden in the undergrowth and almost at her feet. But no, it couldn't be, such a thing could never happen, it couldn't actually be Ben's ball. Transfixed with excitement and disbelief, she couldn't move, she simply couldn't stoop down and see for certain, and then Ben came up and saw it too.

"Why, there it is, staring at you. You are a blind bat!" he said kindly but contemptuously. He picked it up and ran away tossing it in the air.

"I might have found it for him, I could have been the girl who found Ben's ball. It'll never, never happen again, Why didn't I, oh, why?"

She ran blindly into the house, on the way nearly knocking over Mrs Sanderson who, seeing the look on the child's face, was troubled. She had not made much headway with Harriet as yet, although summer was now at hand. On several occasions Margot, with many pretty apologies and expressions of gratitude, had asked her if she would give an eye to Harriet when she and Andrew were going out for the evening. At first Letty had suggested stories and games, but Harriet had so obviously preferred any and every television programme and taking herself off to bed without help at the stipulated time, that she had not persevered. There was no denying that she found Harriet unattractive and unresponsive, a definite disappointment, but, displeased with herself for feeling like this towards the child, she had determined to make a more positive approach one day. Now she decided she would not put this off any longer. The doll's house would be her trump card of course, and yet it was something of an effort to play it. It would be good to rescue it from being a mere museum piece, to witness again a child's delight in the previous object, yet she was conscious of a wish to keep it sacrosanct, secure in the past.

But with the impression of Harriet's stricken look as she had rushed past her, Letty dealt firmly with this sentimental weakness and wrote a note to Margot which she pushed into the Royces' letterbox.

"Harriet," said Margot the next morning. "Mrs Sanderson has kindly invited you to tea today to see her doll's house."

"Doll's houses are for babies," said Harriet indignantly. "The Queensmead one was kept in the nursery and I never played with it even when I was only five."

"Well, it's very kind of Mrs Sanderson anyhow," said

Margot, "and it wouldn't be polite or nice not to go."

"You'll probably get a splendid tea," said Andrew, "Mrs S. did us proud at her party."

Harriet did not reply.

"Don't sulk," said Margot, "it's not as if you get that many invitations to tea. It's about time that you made some little friends at school, isn't it, then you could ask them here and get asked back in return. Meanwhile, of course you must go to Mrs Sanderson's, and when you go, please try and look as though you want to see her doll's house."

So soon after four o'clock, having come back from school and changed from her brown jersey and skirt into her blue velveteen, Harriet knocked on Mrs Sanderson's sitting-room door.

"We'll see the doll's house first, I think," said Mrs Sanderson. "I keep it in my bedroom."

Mrs Sanderson's bedroom looked immense to Harriet — it would have held six of her own little room easily, and at first she didn't see the doll's house, which stood in an alcove which had once held a carving table.

"Here it is," said Mrs Sanderson and stood aside.

"Oh!" exclaimed Harriet, "Oh, but it isn't a doll's house, it's a real house. Why, it's *this* house got little."

"Yes," said Letty, "it's a little Lotus House, and it was made like that cleverly by two nice boys who used to live here once. I'll open it for you so that you can see inside."

Harriet eagerly knelt down in front of it, just as Selina had done long ago on that memorable birthday.

"It's got real furniture in it," she said, "real proper furniture, and pictures on the walls and pots and pans in the kitchen and bedclothes and curtains and little books, and there's people in it!"

"Of course," said Letty, "what did you expect?"

Harriet certainly had not expected anything like this.

59

The silly tiny toy doll's house at Queensmead hadn't any people in it, and only broken bits of plastic tables and chairs. She looked up at Letty and her small dark eyes, so extremely unlike her mother's, were unusually bright and shining.

"May I take the people out and look at them?"

"Yes, if you're careful," said Letty.

"There's a father and a mother and a little girl!" cried Harriet.

"That's Mr and Mrs Golightly and their daughter Wilhelmina Rose — aren't those nice names?"

"No," said Harriet, "they're silly names, I think."

Letty was taken aback and would have felt ridiculously annoyed had she not immediately told herself that this was absurd. It was, of course, for that other child that she felt momentarily hurt, the child who long ago had invented those odd, old, dear names — yet nothing now could touch that child, so why worry?

"What ought they to be called then, do you think?" she asked.

"*I* know," said Harriet. She had known at once but she was not going to tell. "I can see more people, there's an old man in bed — what's he in bed for?"

So then Letty recounted Selina's story of the famous railway disaster. "It happened at the bottom of this very garden," she said.

"It couldn't have," said Harriet, "there's houses there."

Letty explained patiently that the garden used to go right down to the railway; "There was an orchard and a vegetable garden where all the houses are now."

"Oh," said Harriet, not very interested, "well, I don't think there was a railway accident, *I* think he just didn't have any legs ever. Who's that lady in the kitchen? What funny clothes!"

"She's the cook, she's got a cap and an apron on, all cooks used to wear them."

60

But Harriet didn't know about cooks. "Is Miss Cook a relation? She's very like her."

"So she is," agreed Letty. "Now shall we go and have our tea, perhaps you could toast some buns?"

"Yes, I could," said Harriet, getting up slowly from her knees, "but may I come back afterwards?"

"Indeed you may," said Letty, "and if you promise me always to be very careful, you can come and play with the little house by yourself sometimes. I expect Saturdays would be best, when you don't go to school."

"Thank you," said Harriet, "thank you very much."

When the afternoon was over and Harriet had gone, Letty felt pleased on the whole, for Harriet, in spite of her rejection of the whole Golightly saga, had responded satisfactorily to the doll's house in every other way and she felt herself warmed towards the child.

From then onwards Harriet spent most Saturday mornings playing with the little house. She had begun, as every child will do, by rearranging all the furniture, and then settled down to her own particular inventions. The inhabitants led very humdrum lives compared to those they had enjoyed in the past. Letty, though she took care never to interfere or to stay in the room for long, caught snatches from time to time and soon learnt the new names of the late Golightlys: "And how are you this morning, my dear Mrs Royce, and how is your dear husband, Mr Royce, and your darling little daughter Harriet?"

Selina, thought Letty, had been a child who could afford fantasy, the wilder the better: "Oh, no, no, no, Ros, I don't *want* them real."

But now there were no more burglaries or elopements or fires or accidents.

"You shall have this big wardrobe in your bedroom, Harriet, for all the lovely dresses I have bought you. No, of course you need not go to school tomorrow, it's my birthday. Your Mummy couldn't have a birthday with her

61

darling little daughter at school. We'll ask Daddy to come home early and all have a lovely party together . . . " Or, another time: "Look, Harriet darling, Cook has made this cake especially for you, your favourite chocolate icing — would you like to ask your best friend Ben to tea — we'll send a piece up to grandfather, shall we? He'll love to see you — he says you grow more and more like me every day . . . "

These and like snippets of doll's house conversation overheard on Saturday mornings often made Letty Sanderson feel a little uneasy.

Harriet's school took music seriously. This was because it had been lucky enough to find Miss Johnson, the head of the music department, who was an enthusiast and who believed that everyone, given the chance, could develop some measure of musical appreciation and ability. She started all the younger children as soon as they came with singing, recorders, cymbals, whistles and drums. Harriet looked forward to the music sessions and to her astonishment it wasn't long before she had found that she was singled out for praise. One day Miss Johnson told her to stay behind when the class was over and asked her if she would like to have special lessons besides playing in the band. Had she ever thought of learning to play a violin for instance? They wanted some more violin players in the junior orchestra.

Harriet did not speak but her tell-tale face gave Miss Johnson her answer.

"I think you *would* like it," she said.

"Yes," said Harriet, "yes, I would, but I would rather learn the piano, please." Since coming to live at the Lotus House she had often listened to Andrew playing his piano and sometimes it gave her a prickly feeling down her spine which was queer but splendid. Her favourite piece of furniture in the doll's house had always been the little piano and the doll, Harriet, could play it quite well.

"Very well, the piano it shall be," said Miss Johnson, who believed on the whole in putting a pupil's wishes before her own, "I'll write to your mother."

And a day or two later Margot had the letter.

"The school seem to think Harriet is musical," she said to Andrew that evening. "They suggest that she might have piano lessons."

"Good for Harriet," said Andrew.

"Well, I don't know so much, the fees are high enough as it is — I can't afford frills."

"Music isn't a frill," said Andrew.

"Sorry, darling, but you know how mean Dick is, and his wretched parents have never offered to help."

"He's got another family now to support, hasn't he?" said Andrew. "And weren't his parents pretty sick at your leaving him?"

"Why are you defending him suddenly?" said Margot crossly.

"I'm not particularly," said Andrew, "I'm only stating the facts."

"Well, anyway, I think learning the piano will only take her attention and time away from proper lessons and she's backward enough as it is."

"Can I see the letter?" asked Andrew. She tossed it over to him and he read it carefully.

"I'd teach her myself," he said thoughtfully, "only I'd find it difficult to be regular and besides, I'm sure I'm not a good teacher, I know nothing about it. I expect there are all sorts of new methods. Look here, Margot, if you can't manage the extra money, I can."

Margot looked at him curiously. "I suppose I ought to be grateful," she said, "but I rather think you're offering this just to annoy me."

"Don't be silly," said Andrew.

"Well, why this sudden concern for Harriet?"

"I don't think I'm doing it for Harriet exactly."

"Whatever for, then?"

"For music, I suppose," said Andrew slowly.

Margot experienced a dim glimpse at worlds unrealized. She acknowledged, of course, the value of the arts in general. She went to an occasional concert though she knew (but would never have admitted it) that she would not really have wanted a single record on her Desert Island, but would have plumped for eight luxuries instead. She attended picture exhibitions as part of her work assignment and prided herself on her judgement of the monetary value of works of art, and she strove to keep abreast of the most talked-of films, plays and novels. Her furnishings and decorations were always interesting and in fashion, and therefore contained few permanent objects. Andrew's piano was really the only recognizably stable feture in their successive sitting-rooms, also the only one that was there because it was loved. Margot saw, but did not feel, how beautiful things were. She did not understand what Andrew meant about music, but Harriet got her lessons.

"Are you going to let the child practise on your precious piano?" asked Margot incredulously, for it soon became clear that practising at school wasn't enough for either Miss Johnson or Harriet.

"Yes, I think so," said Andrew, "not when I'm working at home, of course, and never with sticky fingers." He smiled at Harriet, "But I'm sure you'll see to that, Harriet, won't you?"

"Yes, I will," said Harriet.

"Now darling," Mrs Doll's House Royce said to her little girl, "you must practise regularly every single day and you must never, never forget to wash your hands *most* properly first."

CHAPTER SIX

ALL THROUGH THE winter and spring Mrs Sanderson had difficulty in procuring any reliable domestic help. The Lotus House was not the type to attract these rare specimens, especially her own rooms with their wide expanses of floorboards needing polishing (she disliked fitted carpets) and actually with two antiquated open fireplaces. Helps arrived, drank a great deal of her tea or coffee according to taste, disapproved and disappeared. The latest had been a chain-smoker and had left trails of ash all over the place. Letty at last decided to tackle her, not because of the ash, nor for the smell of stale smoke which was unpleasantly difficult to get rid of, but about the dangers of lung cancer. She feared that any advice might be taken as interference but the girl was so young and it did seem a pity. Her gentle remonstrance however was not resented nor was it of any use.

"Well, what I say is, we've all got a date fixed." And she in her turn vanished without any warning.

"You're looking quite worn out, Mrs Sanderson," said Miss Budgeon at the little corner shop. Letty bought all her fruit and vegetables there now.

"Oh, it's nothing. I get rather tired sometimes, that's all. I haven't any help at present." Miss Budgeon looked thoughtful.

Three days later a smart slim car deposited an equally

smart slim passenger at the Lotus House who rang Letty's bell. She was heavily made-up and wore a black silk blouse, tight scarlet trousers and matching scarlet stilletto heeled shoes.

"Mrs Sanderson?" enquired this vision crisply. "I'm Dian — she said at the shop you needed help, dear, and I think I can fit you in Tuesdays."

Letty gazed at her in astonishment. How could Miss Budgeon have possibly thought this black and scarlet dragonfly suitable for cleaning floors and scrubbing woodwork? Still, there she stood waiting.

"Thank you very much," murmured Letty, "but you'd better have a look round first, I think."

The look round, however, did not apparently disconcert Dian.

"Righty ho, then," she said when it was finished. "I'll be here Tuesday next, ten sharp." The car drove off.

"*She* won't last long," commented Letty to herself, "if she ever turns up at all."

Tuesday morning however, brought Dian all right, and in the self-same clothes, the only concession she made to her morning's work was to change her stilettos into a pair of equally smart sandals tied on with velvet ribbon, and to envelop herself in an overall of shocking pink.

It did not take long however for Letty to discover that Miss Budgeon had provided her with a treasure. Never had floorboards shone so, never had rugs and carpets looked so trim, never had tiles and taps twinkled so brightly. Dian was both quick and thorough — floors were her passion. She seldom seemed to look above the skirting-board in the sitting-room and bedrooms, but as the dusting was Letty's business, this did not really matter. Objects didn't interest Dian but after her floors had been attended to, she had plenty of observation for the people who walked on them.

"That Mrs Royce — she's a peach, she is. I wouldn't

much want my Luke to set eyes on her."

"Your basement, she's a shy one — puts me in mind of a goldfish we've got, slips away behind his waterweed at a shadow."

"Who does for your third-floor then? Doesn't often do to let men do for themselves, dearie — regular messers, most of 'em."

There might be something in this, Letty thought, and after a word with Aubrey Stacey, who seemed grateful, it was arranged that Dian should see to his floor too. "And quite time I should say, thick with dust you could write yer name on, but that vacuum of his came out of the Ark, I shouldn't wonder." Letty had a pleasant momentary vision of Mrs Noah busily at work.

Doing for Aubrey meant that Dian brought her lunch now and stayed on for an extra hour afterwards. Letty and she had the meal together. Dian obviously had never entertained any other idea for a moment but she refused to share Letty's food.

"Must keep to me diet, dearie — it don't matter for you but my Luke likes me sheer." Letty felt uncomfortable consuming her quite substantial lunch, while Dian pecked at two slices of Ryvita spread with a non-fat cream cheese, and nibbled at an apple. She hoped Luke persuaded her to cook for two in the evenings. Luke was another shock when she met him. He was a huge coal-black Jamaican, a junior partner, so Dian proudly boasted, in a garage in Deptford — hence, Letty supposed, the succession of cars that brought Dian every Tuesday morning.

"I don't have to oblige," said Dian, "my Luke brings in good money, but staying at home all day gives me the creeps." Luke and Dian lived on the estate but though so near, Dian never walked if she could avoid it. Sometimes, even, Luke would call again for her and take her back home. He had other uses too.

The delivery of Miss Cook's post was a constant source of annoyance to her. The postman insisted on ignoring her prized separate entrance and delivered her letters with all the others at the main door. Not that she had much in the way of post, but when she had, it meant that she either had to fetch it or be beholden to Mrs Sanderson or one of the other lodgers for bringing it round and Miss Cook did not care for this. One Tuesday it was Dian who came to her door with a sales catalogue and a picture postcard of Hastings from her sister-in-law Doris, where she and Henry were having a little break. Miss Cook could not refrain from complaint.

"It's too bad, causing all this trouble, what's he paid for, I'd like to know?"

"Well, it's only natural really," said Dian, "it's the same name, 'The Lotus House'. Pretty, I call it."

"But it's got 'The Basement Flat' written perfectly clearly," said Miss Cook, "and I've told him again and again."

"Not to worry," said Dian, "I'll get my Luke to have a word with him — my Luke, he's known all round here. Mind if I have a look at your catalogue? What they get up to these days!" she added, "You're in luck, luv, see what it says here," and she started to read out very slowly: " 'You have been chosen to take part in our very special draw, limited to only a few customers, and I have some more exciting news for you, Miss Cook. You have been selected to receive one of the superb gifts pictured on page 5 of our catalogue. All you have to do is to return your lucky number with your order.' Oo, let's look at page 5."

"It's all nonsense," said Miss Cook, "it's just to make you buy their stuff which I never have. I don't know how they got hold of my name."

"But they aren't all cons," said Dian, "my Luke he knows a fellow, met him standing drinks all round at the

Green Man one night, he'd won a Metro with his lucky number, red it was Luke said, he saw it there outside in the car park, brand-new all right, 's truth. Mind you, it's your stars as does it and they don't oblige often, but you never know do you — that's what I like about life really, you never know. Which one of them superb gifts will you choose, then?"

"I don't want any of them," said Miss Cook, sniffing contemptuously, "thank you for bringing round my post," and she moved purposefully towards the door.

"Goldfish," sighed Dian to herself and retreated. But Janet Cook had no more trouble about her letters.

"Postman behaving himself?" enquired Dian, "I says as my Luke'd fix him," and it wasn't long after this that Janet had a further greater reason to be grateful to Dian's Luke.

All the estate children were a source of irritation to Janet. Their shouting and screaming and shrill laughter (of all noises except perhaps the barking of dogs, the ugliest and most disturbing), this she was prepared to put up with as the unenviable snag which she had expected to discover when first moving into this otherwise pleasant new home. But the behaviour of "the Terribles" went beyond this (that of course was only Harriet's private name for them, but it was one of which Janet would have approved). On one occasion it even menaced her personal safety, or so she was convinced.

As winter had given place to spring, Janet Cook had begun to cultivate her strip of garden. Obsessively conscientious by upbringing, she took her responsibility for this seriously but also, unsuspected by herself, she happened to have inherited from her country clergyman grandfather something of more value than his armchair or the tradition of gentility so treasured by her mother. He had loved growing things and had possessed green fingers. Janet had always had a weakness for flowers and had not infrequently incurred her mother's rebukes for squandering her money on them. Now she purchased a paperback on gardening, several packets of seeds from Woolworth's, a trowel, a fork and a pair of gardening gloves. She had set herself to clear the ground so that she could sow her seeds, and they had grown splendidly — but so had the weeds. She was emptying her bucket of these on the compost heap among the old bushes by the fence one day just as 'the Terribles' rushed out in a body and started to use the fence as a target. *Pop, bang, pop* went their peashooters, making Janet jump so that she upset her weeds all over the place. One bullet came over and nearly hit her.

"Stop that at once!" she called out. Immediately heads appeared above the fence.

"Get along, you old cow," shouted out one boy.

"Let's see if we can hit her bucket," shouted another, "if she gets peppered it's her own bloody fault."

Janet trembled with rage but just then Dian appeared, it being Tuesday, to shake out the ground-floor rugs.

"Look out," called out one of the boys, "it's big Luke's trout," and all the heads disappeared.

Janet picked up her basket, she was still trembling at the outrage.

"What's them boys bin up to?" said Dian. "They get above themselves sometimes. Mind you it's their Mums' and Dads' fault. You and me was brought up different."

"I should think so!" exclaimed Janet Cook. "I shall complain to the police."

"Oh, I wouldn't do that, really," said Dian, "My Luke'll see to them, they'll mind him better 'n any policemen." Janet, recollecting the postman and considering how rapidly the Terribles had disappeared, was inclined to believe her and, true enough, she was free of insults from that day. Feeling under an obligation to Dian, she actually decided to invite her in for a cup of tea on one of her Tuesdays. Dian accepted with alacrity. She looked appreciatively round the flat.

"It's real cosy, I wonder Mrs Sanderson didn't take it for herself, instead of them great fancy rooms of hers."

Janet was gratified. "It isn't just as I want it yet though," she said. "I'm saving up for a new carpet." *Now why have I told her that*, she thought, *it's none of her business*.

But Dian nodded in quick sympathy. "I favour them as suck your feet in like, as if you were walking in a bog," she said, "Luke and me'll buy one of those when we win the pools. But this one's a nice colour though. Tell you what, mind if I bring along me new shampoo? Got it as a sample last week. What you can get nowadays! Free it was, 'cept for the stamps. It brought mine up lovely."

The shampoo certainly did make a difference and the two women shared the pleasure of achievement and another cup of tea together.

"In spite of her looks and the way she speaks, I believe she really has a heart of gold," Janet said to that persistently admonishing voice of her mother, undeterred apparently by the grave, "and her Luke has been most useful. Yes, Mother, I know he is black, but I can't help that and nor can he, and whatever grandfather would say, he's been a real help."

Miss Cook soon had another worry. A mouse actually ventured into the kitchen of the basement flat. "I never thought to have had mice *here*," she exclaimed outraged to Letty, who found herself apologizing humbly.

"I wouldn't have thought it either," she said, "especially in *your* kitchen, Miss Cook."

Janet abominated mice. They were dirty, destructive and noisy — "How anyone can say 'as quiet as a mouse', I can't imagine, and they dart about so, it unnerves me."

"It's primeval," said Dian darkly, "you can't do nothing

about what's primeval — except traps."

"I can't bear dealing with traps," said Janet. There had been mice and traps at intervals in Albert Street, but her mother or Henry had always dealt with them.

"Traps is cruel," agreed Dian, "well, there's cats, they're more natural, and leastways the cat gets some fun."

"I don't really want to be bothered with a cat," said Janet. "We never were a family for pets."

"Well," said Dian, "it's traps or cats or mice, 'cause it won't stop by itself. Cats is the most lasting and reliable I'd say."

They were talking at Miss Cook's door, and just at that moment the fugitive cat which Harriet had once seen escaping from the Terribles streaked across the lawn again. She had appeared several times before this and Miss Cook had always shooed her away. She started now to shoo once more but Dian stopped her. "It's sent all right, fancy that — it's milk, not shooing, you ought to be after."

"What do you mean," said Miss Cook affronted. "Who's sent it?"

"It's your stars as sent it, Miss Cook," replied Dian solemnly.

"Do you really think I should encourage it?" said Janet doubtfully.

"If you wants to get rid of that mouse," said Dian.

"But what about its owners?"

"Don't worry yourself about *them*," snorted Dian, "till they worries you, which'll be never, see? It's starving, that poor cat is, anyone can see with half an eye. A saucer or two of milk and it'll be yours for life. That poor kid upstairs'll be pleased, too, I bet."

Dian was right about Harriet, who met the cat in the garden the next day and recognized it at once. Miss Cook was busy gardening.

72

"Is she your cat, then?" asked Harriet, "I didn't think she was yours."

"She is now," said Miss Cook grudgingly, "she kept coming over from the estate to get away from those boys."

"Oh, I *know*,' said Harriet, "I am so glad she's your cat now, what are you going to call her?"

Janet hadn't thought of calling her anything but "Puss". "But 'Puss' is every cat's surname," objected Harriet, "I shall call her 'Maisie'." Maisie had been the name of a beautiful aristocratic white Persian with blue eyes who lived next door to Queensmead, and who had reminded Harriet of her mother.

"Do you mind if she is called Maisie?" she asked anxiously.

"You can call her what you like," answered Miss Cook rather shortly. She had no special objection to Harriet who had not shown herself to be a snag as yet, but she did not want to encourage her to come chattering, nor to have her bothering round after the cat, so she did not continue the conversation but picked up her trowel and went indoors and Maisie followed her. "She doesn't like me," thought Harriet, "but she's kind, she likes Maisie."

Letty Sanderson learned more about her tenants from her Tuesday lunch times with Dian than from her own observations. She told herself she ought to stop Dian from gossiping but this was next to impossible, and it was also, it must be confessed, very tempting to listen. What she heard was sometimes disquieting and she wished she need not believe it, but Dian was so transparently and objectively honest, she found she had to.

"That Aubrey, he's a queer, I'd say, but not one of them jolly ones, if you know what I mean — too many bottles about, but no one to share 'em with, is there?"

Mrs Sanderson confirmed that Mr Stacey seemed to

have few friends and Dian nodded. "I'd know if there'd been a party."

"Mr Stacey spends his leisure-time writing," said Letty firmly, "He's an author."

"I dessay," said Dian, "poor chap!"

Letty smiled but the thought of the bottles haunted her all the same.

In addition to doing the rough work for Mrs Sanderson and Aubrey, Dian had sometimes obliged Margot when she had an extra work-load.

"You can't resist her, can you," she said, "but I don't get satisfaction out of all that matting she has on the floors, it's not homely. But that Margot, she'd make a fortune on the telly, I tells her — she's got what it takes right enough. Funny her taking up with that Andrew, regular stick he is, might be one of they computers doing all the work for all he cares, he don't see me even if I'm right under his nose, which I have to be as often as not, for he don't move an inch for the vacuum to get out of me way."

"But he notices his wife, I hope," Letty couldn't help saying a little anxiously.

"You bet," said Dian, "but mind you, if it came to busting up, he'd get along without her better nor the other way round."

"Well, it won't come to that, I'm sure," said Letty decisively. She really mustn't let herself discuss such matters with Dian. But it was no use.

"You never know these days," said Dian cheerfully, "and especially when there's never been any wedding bells neither."

"But Dian," said Letty shocked, "what makes you say that? I know Mrs Royce uses her first husband's name still for her business purposes, perhaps that has muddled you."

She was dreadfully afraid that she saw Dian wink.

74

"What does she want with a business, anyways?" she said, "Of course, if it was the telly, it would be different, but her's is just a shop. My mum now, she had to leave us, my Dad got hisself killed in the war, see, but she made it up to us when she was at home, like one of them old boilers she was, stoked up early mornings and evenings so that it warms you all day long."

"But you go out to work and you say you don't have to," said Letty.

"I haven't a kid to look after," said Dian, "that Harriet, she's no better than a latchkey child, I wouldn't oblige as I do if I'd had a little kid." She was silent for a moment. "My Luke, he'd've liked one too, but I guess I was too old when I took up with him. Anyways, time to clear them bottles out of that attic now — tootle-oo, luv," and she disappeared up the stairs.

CHAPTER SEVEN

A YEAR HAD passed since Letty Sanderson had moved into the Lotus House. Miss Cook's efforts had produced a flourishing row of sweetpeas and clumps of drowsy-smelling stocks. These had given place to marigolds and red dwarf dahlias — the latter were expensive but she had been assured that after the first frost, if she dug them up and stored them for replanting in May, they would last her for a long while. The first frosts were late that year and the garden was bright till the end of October.

To Harriet the time she lived in the Lotus House seemed very long. She was still at an age when the past scarcely exists in the conscious mind and the future is too vague to intrude on the all-important present. Childhood is a violent period — an hour of misery or of happiness has no conceivable end. Time has not yet learnt its confines, eternity lies in wait for us at every corner.

For Letty, of course, it was the other way round. The year had flown by and as she grew older, time went so fast that the present was hardly to be caught and pinned down. It was like trying to lay hold of a dream before it vanishes into the light of the real world. And which was the reality, she sometimes wondered?

It was All Hallows day.

"Do you believe in ghosts?" Dian enquired of Miss Cook.

"No," said Janet, "certainly not."

"Luke and me do," said Dian, "Luke, he's seen things hisself, in other countries mind, not here, and there's plenty of people on the telly that's seen them."

Janet sniffed.

"But I wonder," went on Dian, "why are they always sad or wicked? Aren't there any happy and good ones?"

"There aren't any at all," said Janet firmly, "but if there were, the good ones'd have something better to do, I should say, than to hang around here."

"Well, but you'd think they'd like to come and see how we was getting on. I know I would if it was Luke was left, and the places where I'd enjoyed myself, too. P'raps there *are* nice ghosts but they don't get talked about. People'd think them soft, I dessay, and they wouldn't make a good telly programme, see. That's it, I expect. I like 'em best wicked myself — the sort that lure you on."

"What nonsense," commented Janet Cook to herself. She had somehow fallen into the habit of inviting Dian in for a cup of tea quite frequently on her Tuesdays. After the rescue from 'the Terribles', it had seemed polite so to do, and then actually pleasant. She was surprised at herself but there it was. Having a place of your own was so different, and Dian was appreciative, no doubt of that.

"Looks lovely now your carpet does; funny how much bigger your lounge looks than Luke's and mine though I bet it's smaller really, we're so crowded up. My Luke's a collector, see, all sorts of things. I tell him he hasn't left space enough to swing a kitten, let alone a cat. Talk of the devil, here's that Maisie at the window now."

"She's not allowed in here," said Janet.

"Looks as if she's in the family way," said Dian.

"Oh dear, do you think so? I hope not," exclaimed Janet. "Isn't it just that she was so thin before and you're noticing the difference?"

Dian shook her head. "She's plumped out all right but

it's all in one place. You should have got her seen to."

"I never thought. I don't know much about these things," said Janet.

"Well, it's too late now," said Dian cheerfully, "and anyways, I expect it'd be shutting the stable door after that Mrs Bates' Blackie had got at her. She's never had *him* done and never will and he's a regular Donje."

"A what?" asked Janet.

"A Donje, a Spanisher he was, and a sugar daddy if ever there was one. They Spanishers are worse than any my Luke says, and he's travelled all over the place, used to be a stoker, see."

Maisie was pressed against the window pane glowering at them balefully. Janet was determined that she should remain strictly a working kitchen-cat, but Maisie was equally convinced that by rights she had now attained the status of a drawing-room pet. She had somehow become "Maisie" to everyone, though Janet disapproved of animals being given the names of human beings.

"Will it be soon?" she enquired.

"Not so long, I'd say," said Dian, eyeing Maisie speculatively, "but you'll know it's when she starts to look about the place, see."

"What will she be looking for?"

"Her maternity bed," said Dian, "and it'll be no sort of use your giving her a box or basket, never mind if it's got ever so nice a cushion in it or anything. Cats are that choosy, no National Health for them, see, private and special, just what takes their fancy. My mum's Rosy, she had her first lot in my sister's bottom drawer, nipped in when no one was looking, Sis not shutting it proper after she'd been showing off her wedding veil. For her next she fancied Gran's cardigan — the one she kept for best. Then it was my Dad's box of picture papers — hoards 'em up he does for rainy days, but Rosie, she tore 'em all to bits, so then Dad had her seen to and Mum said she wished it had been her, 'cause there was five of us already, see, and another on the way, no pill then there wasn't and Mum careless, but she didn't mean nothing, she loved us all every one she did, and no one was to know my Dad was going to get hisself killed."

"Well," said Janet, "I shall take good care this cat is shut out from now on. I shall continue to feed her, of course, but she must not be allowed in — after all she's only a stray."

Sometimes Dian rattled on in a way that re-awakened in Janet Cook that disapproving voice, grown somewhat fainter of late; "This is not at all the sort of person to invite into your home, not a fit acquaintance for you, Janet."

All the same, she heard herself actually accepting a return invitation to visit Dian that very next week.

"It's a terrible early supper, Luke comes home that hungry. You won't mind, will you, dear?" said Dian.

Afterwards Janet Cook wondered why she hadn't made up some excuse to refuse, but it was difficult with Dian somehow, the mistake, she feared, was having got on such terms in the first place, as her mother kept tiresomely reminding her. Yet she found herself looking forward to the visit. It must be confessed she was curious to see Dian's home and to meet Luke, for, what with the move to the Lotus House and the garden and getting to know Dian, a strange new sensation had recently invaded her — an urge, faint but persistent, towards adventure.

Dian and Luke lived in one of the estate houses and outside it looked no different from its neighbours, but when the front door opened Janet Cook was confronted with something disconcertingly different. Facing her was a large wooden plaque on which was emblazoned in ornamental poker work the words:

Welcome All

To Happy Hall.

On the reverse side it said:

Don't miss your train
But come again.

Surrounding this and decorating the passage were flags of many different nations. A door painted a brilliant blue led into quite a large room, but as Dian had said, it did not look its size. Its walls were covered from top to toe with matchboxes of all sizes, shapes and colours, strung together in long festoons. In front of each of the two windows were stands crowded with flourishing pot plants. Above the mantelpiece were two more pokerwork plaques — one declared that "East, West, home is best", and the other "Good food, good drink, good cheer, Good health to all folks here". Beneath, one of those electric fires of mock glowing coal was flanked each side by a gnome sitting on a large red and white toadstool. In the centre of the room was a round table covered with dishes; two fat red plush chairs and a conch found space for themselves somehow, and in one corner was an outsize television set crowned with framed family photographs. In the other a guitar propped itself against a goldfish bowl.

Janet Cook, staring about her with her sharp black eyes, was quite taken aback by all this odd miscellany.

"See what I mean?" said Dian, "I don't care so much for objects myself, but Luke, he's a collector like I said, and he's that good about dusting all his boxes hisself."

"You've got some lovely plants," said Janet politely.

"Not half bad," agreed Dian, "though I says it. I have to have 'em all in here, there's no sort of use trying to grow 'em in the garden, see."

Janet looked out of the window and indeed did see that the garden also was very full, but not of flowers or vegetables. A great many more gnomes made a bright border to a patch of grass which was populated by a

80

number of large and small tortoises, perambulating slowly round in search of the lettuce leaves strewn about for their benefit.

"Luke, he loves them tortoises," explained Dian, "he can't bear for to see 'em in those pet shops, crawling all over each other, dying and sad. I tell him the more he buys 'em up, the more the dealers'll get others in, but it don't carry no weight with him. He says as it won't make no difference to speak of to the trade but it'll make all the difference in the world to these here tortoises now, but he'll have to stop soon, 'cause there won't be any more room for 'em. Same with the gnomes, he buys 'em plain and colours 'em hisself, he can't keep off 'em; they gnomes and they tortoises, they're like children to him, and he feels almost as much for Fred, that's the goldfish. I can't get up enthusiasm for 'im myself. Won 'im in a raffle, I did, for cancer research — well, you never know, do you? I wanted a mink coat and I got a goldfish. Still, he don't give us trouble. That's Luke now, it's his boxing night really, but he said he'd give it a miss so as to come back early to meet you. He's a super boxer, is Luke, that's why the boys mind him."

Luke was enormous. When Janet Cook saw him filling up the doorway, she wondered how on earth he could fit into the crowded sitting-room, but he moved around with a slow sureness. He extinguished Dian in a huge hug from which she extricated herself as if used to it. Then he turned to Janet and seized her limp unready hand and worked it up and down like a pump handle.

"What have you got for us to eat then, darling?" he asked Dian.

"He's always afraid I'm going to starve him," she said.

"She starves herself, not me," said Luke to Janet. "Looks like there's plenty on the table anyways. Why, that's my gal, she don' forget her ole man."

"You don't have to taste them, if you don't want," said

Dian to Janet, "sweet potatoes and kidney beans, that's what Luke likes, but I never touch 'em — it's what you're used to, isn't it?"

Janet Cook, sitting bolt upright on the edge of her chair, nibbled at a paste sandwich and a piece of chocolate roll, and watched Luke as if he were some strange animal as he worked his way steadily through plateful after plateful. But at last he finished and began to talk. He had a soft warm voice.

"You like my matchboxes, honey?" he enquired.

"It must have taken you a very long time to collect them all," Janet replied evasively.

"Ever since I was a little 'un," said Luke, "I used to ask the sailors for them when they put in at the harbour. I was raised in Old Spanish Town and I were mad after the sea, went as a cabin boy soon as I were old enough, then got to be stoker — trading in bananas, we were, and everywhere we went I got them matchboxes. But one day come and I'd enough of wandering, was that the day I met my darling? Near enough. Then it was 'East, West, home's best', wasn't it, honey? But I kept my matchboxes."

"Give us a song, now," said Dian, "he sings lovely, as good as one of they pop guys any day."

Luke took down his guitar and bent over it lovingly.

"Sing 'To my donkey'," ordered Dian, and he began crooning softly. It sounded like a foreign language to Janet. "Tie meh dongdey."

"Now 'Yellow bird'," said Dian. The low rich voice crooned on and Janet Cook's stiff little body relaxed. Then the song changed again.

"This is his favourite," whispered Dian, "it's 'This is my island in the sun' ". Janet had never been out of England and had scarcely ever even seen the sea, but, as she listened, she felt as if she were lying by it — a very blue sea, with scarlet blossoming trees growing close to the shore and brilliant yellow and green birds darting among them.

When Luke stopped singing Janet stood up to leave and Luke said he would see her home. "There's no need for that, thank you," said Janet, but Luke took no notice. Crossing the street he put his arm round her to steer her through the traffic. This made her feel queer and uncomfortable, and she was glad when they reached the Lotus House. Left alone she suddenly realized that she was tired and sat still doing nothing for a little while.

"Well, it takes all sorts," said Janet Cook to herself. And then, "Perhaps I might take one of those coach trips down to the sea one day." And then "Wouldn't like all those matchboxes about, and the tortoises, rather her than me." And then "Wonder what it's like to be her, all the same." She didn't remember ever having been hugged and hardly kissed even, since those hurried embraces from poor old Dad years and years ago — you couldn't call those pecks she and her mother exchanged "kisses". "They say you don't miss what you've never had — I liked the singing, though."

She sat for a bit longer. Then, "Mustn't be fanciful," she said, and got up to take off her jacket and put away her bag.

The next morning brought a letter from her sister-in-law. *Wonder what she wants*, she thought. Contacts between them were usually confined to a picture postcard on holidays and birthdays and Christmas greetings. The letter said that Doris (now second mistress in the large primary school of the very respectable suburb where she and Henry had their home), had been asked to deputize for her headmistress at an important educational conference in the north where her parents lived, and she had obtained extra leave of absence to extend her stay for a week so as to visit them. "We thought it might make a nice change for you to keep Henry company while I am

83

away. You have never seen our new house," Doris wrote.

"No, because this is the first time you have asked me to visit you since Mother died and you moved," said Janet, "It's as plain as a pikestaff you want me just to cook and clean while you're not there. How do they know I want a nice change? I don't, as a matter of fact. Pretty sure of me, too, Doris is, gives me times of trains and bus connections, not going to get the car out for me, no fear. Still, blood is thicker than water and I shall go, I suppose."

She duly gave Mrs Sanderson her spare key, packed her small neat suitcase, and set off on the day and at the hour suggested by Doris, who opened the door to her.

"Quite a walk from the bus stop," observed Janet, "further than the other house."

"The Avenue's a much better neighbourhood," said Doris. "We owe it to Henry's promotion — you knew of that, of course?"

"Of course," said Janet. "A bit overdue, wasn't it?"

Doris eyed her sister-in-law sharply. She was a tall rather imposing woman, still handsome, with regular features and large brown protruding eyes behind her spectacles, but her face was lined and Janet thought she looked distinctly older than when she had last seen her.

"Where's Henry?" she enquired.

"He's washing down the car," said Doris, "it's a new one and he's very careful of it. I expect you got a cup of tea on the journey."

"No," said Janet, "there was no opportunity."

"Oh, well, it's a bit late now, isn't it, and we have supper early. Come into the lounge."

The lounge was a long narrow room with windows at both ends. It struck Janet as cold, for it was one of those days when rain is in the offing and there is too much wind about. If she had been at home she would have switched her fire full on. The pale grey walls, empty of pictures,

84

and the dark green covers and curtains gave her the shivers.

"I'm glad I stood out against Doris and got pink for mine," she thought. Then Henry appeared. He had the same small tight mouth as his sister and the same sharp black eyes, but his face was pale with a long chin and, whereas her hair was still black and thick, his was grey and brushed in careful thin strands across his head.

"'And he's three years younger than I am," said Janet to herself with satisfaction. He began to tell her about the new car in which she was not interested. Supper, when it came, consisted of a cheese soufflé that didn't allow of second helpings, salad and fruit.

"We find a light supper much healthier and I know you have trouble with your digestion," said Doris. "We don't take coffee in the evenings, we find it keeps us awake, but I can make some for you if you like."

"I'd like a cup of tea," said Janet. Doris did not move for a moment.

Henry said, "I'll make it dear, you've had a heavy day."

They spent the rest of the evening looking at the television news and then at a travel film of wild life at Spitsbergen, until Janet, who was getting colder and colder, said she would like to go to bed.

"Oh," said Doris, "I don't usually switch on the heater so early, so I'm afraid there's no hot water yet, but I'll heat a jug from the kitchen for you."

Janet took a long while to warm up in bed and even then she did not sleep well. The room smelt musty and unused and she had not opened the window because it was now raining outside, and moreover she had reached the age when a strange bed took getting used to. Also she was hungry. But she slept at last, and then of course did not wake when she should have done and was late down for breakfast. The coffee was tepid and the toast had gone limp and she had disapproving looks from Doris who said:

85

"Henry has had to leave, I'm afraid, I would have called you if you had asked, I've got to catch an early train too. I've left notes about the housekeeping by the phone; we have weekly accounts with the grocer and butcher and Mrs Binns, my help, comes on Wednesday morning to clean — there shouldn't be any difficulties. Henry's got a Conservative Association meeting tomorrow night. I expect you'd like to go with him." (*And I expect I wouldn't*, thought Janet.) "And there's a W.I. lecture on peasant embroidery on Thursday," continued Doris, "you'd be welcome there I know, and the park is nice and handy for walks."

Doris's habit of arranging other people's lives for them always irritated Janet; aloud she said "Oh, I'm used to amusing myself, you needn't worry."

As soon as Doris had left, Janet went into the lounge with the newspaper and switched on all the bars of the electric fire. When it stopped raining she went out shopping and bought herself a hot-water bottle. She also bought a nice piece of beefsteak at the butchers. "People get indigestion just as much from eating too little as too much, and Henry looks as though he could do with a good supper for once." There had been nothing to drink either, the previous evening, so she bought a bottle of sherry. She went to sleep, hugging her hot-water bottle for the whole of the afternoon.

When Henry came home that night she produced the sherry. His eyebrows went up when he saw it.

"Not to worry," said Janet, "it's a present, I noticed you were out."

"Well," said Henry, "actually we had a few friends in the night before you came and we don't usually treat ourselves, got to keep the housekeeping down for a bit."

"Why," said Janet, "I thought you and Doris were both getting more now."

"A little," conceded Henry, "but there's the mortgage,

86

houses in the Avenue are expensive you know; and the car — we had to have a decent one; and Doris thinks we should take our holiday abroad this year. Our neighbours — he's on the Stock Exchange, really nice people, Janet, you must meet them — they're going to Majorca, we rather thought we'd try there too."

Janet did not meet these desirable neighbours after all because Henry made no move towards the introduction, but she spent her time quite pleasantly not doing all the things her sister-in-law had suggested, and providing what she felt were really good meals, and roasting herself before the electric fire, for it remained cold.

"It won't matter for a week," she thought as she ordered a prime cut of lamb and bought a carton of cream to have with the chocolate mousse she had made. She also replenished the sherry, this time not at her own expense. "They'll be paying three times as much for trash at that hotel of theirs in Majorca without blinking an eyelid, I bet. Anyway, I think all this saving and scraping behind the scenes is silly — just to put on a show — that expensive car, don't tell me it's paid for yet. It's Doris — no, that's not fair, I can see it's Henry too — Mother always pushed him more than me and it's just taken this turn." Generations of hard-working honest forefathers stirred in her blood: "Well, I shan't get my new carpet till I can put down every penny's worth."

In the middle of the week Mrs Binns arrived to clean. She was a small, dim little woman with a stutter and seemed upset at being a little late.

"I'm s-sorry, Miss Cook, but this morning our old cat had kittens and I had to s-see to them."

"Oh," said Janet, "what did you do about them?"

"D-drowned them," said Mrs Binns, "that's why I'm late. You have to drown them quick — they don't feel nothing then."

Janet registered this useful piece of information. But

Mrs Binns was no Dian and they had no further conversation, though she seemed surprised and grateful for a bountiful elevenses.

Henry and Janet did not talk much in the evenings but then they never had. On the last night before Doris returned, they watched a travel film together because it was about Majorca, but you didn't see much of the country — it was mostly of the hotels and people eating and drinking and dancing, all of which looks much the same wherever it's done. Then there was the news and then a programme on immigrants, which Henry switched off almost at once.

"A great mistake ever to have let them in," he said.

"But they've got to live somewhere," said Janet.

"Not here, they haven't," said Henry, "all these blacks and gypsies, too, rascals and scroungers the lot. Do you know, Janet, they even talk of a gypsy site on a disused railway property within walking distance of the Avenue. It'll be the blacks next — you have to fight for a decent society all the time nowadays, I don't know what the country's coming to."

Janet looked at him. She had never noticed before how like their mother he was. The spirit of opposition which he and Doris often aroused in her flared up. For a moment or two she had a vision of the cold grey walls of Doris' lounge festooned with coloured matchboxes and flags, and it improved them.

"Well, I think it makes life more interesting not to be all the same," she said.

Henry frowned. "You've changed, Janet," he said accusingly, "I've been thinking so all the week. What's come over you? Don't think I haven't noticed how much the housekeeping books must have gone up with what you've spent, and now these notions. I don't know what our mother would say."

Yes, you do, thought Janet, *and it would be just the*

same as you. But she was a little shaken all the same. She went to bed that night wondering if she *had* changed and she felt uncomfortably sure that Henry was right — this was a bit frightening. She fell asleep with her mother's, or Henry's voice (it didn't matter which) chanting over and over again, softly but insistently, like an unpleasant lullaby, "You can't be too careful."

Meanwhile, at the Lotus House, Maisie had had her kittens. Being denied entry to her rightful territory, she had made do with the tool-shed which had a convenient window and a not too inadequate pile of sacking in a corner. There Letty found her, the proud mother of five as far as she could see. She wished Miss Cook had left instructions about what she wanted done with them. "I ought to have asked — I am getting forgetful — I've noticed it lately." For the moment however she did nothing but fetch Maisie a large saucer of milk. *Anyway she's due back tomorrow*, she thought, and forgot about it again.

But in the afternoon she was disturbed by a flushed and agitated Harriet bursting into her sitting-room without even knocking.

"Oh, Mrs Sanderson, come quickly," she cried, "poor, poor Maisie, she's in the tool-shed being bitten dreadfully by lots of horrid rats."

Letty stared at her and then began to laugh. "Oh, Harriet, they're not rats, they're her kittens, she's feeding them."

Harriet didn't believe her, she stamped her foot: "They're not kittens, they're horrible little rats."

"Come along," said Letty, "come and look again."

Maisie greeted them with a roaring purr. "Listen," said Letty, "don't you hear and see how pleased she is?"

Harriet could not deny the purr. "But kittens are pretty and fluffy little things, why should poor Maisie have such ugly kittens? And they've got no eyes," she added horrified.

89

"These will be pretty and fluffy very soon, and their eyes will open," said Letty. "All kittens are like this when they are born. I must say they are rather like rats; but look, this one is going to be a tabby like Maisie, you can see the markings, and three are black, and this one black and white."

Harriet bent over and Maisie gazed up at her proudly, still purring. Then Harriet put out a finger and touched one of the kittens very gently.

"I'm so sorry, Maisie," Letty heard her whisper, "I'm very sorry I thought your children were rats."

Janet Cook arrived home the following evening. She felt a new and definite pleasure as she walked up from the station to the Lotus House. For one thing, it was really a relief to have left Doris and Henry, especially as for the last twenty-four hours she had certainly been under a cloud. She had felt she could not go before Doris returned, that would have looked queer, and Doris had not arrived back until late in the evening.

She was very full of all her doings at the conference. "Might have been running it," commented Janet silently, "thought she was too, I bet, another Maggie Thatcher, that's what she thinks she is."

Then, after Doris and Henry had been alone together, while Janet was getting ready for supper, the cloud had come down, the cloud under which Janet had to finish the evening, pack her bag the next morning, eat a sparse last meal, bid her farewells and take herself off. "Never seen the inside of that car once and probably never will." But besides the shaking off of the cloud, there was the warm anticipation of her own little flat again and her own garden border. The house at Albert Street had simply been her parents' home and an unloved one at that. It had never welcomed anyone. Now she felt a definite welcome as she opened her door and there was even actually a "Welcome Home" card from Dian lying on her mat. *Nice*

90

of her, thought Janet, *nice I'm sure*. But there was also a note from Mrs Sanderson, and when she had read this she was not so pleased. It enclosed her spare key and told her that Maisie had had her kittens and they were in the tool-shed.

Drat the animal, thought Janet, *I suppose I shall have to bother with her now, but I'm going to have a cup of tea first*. She was tired after her journey and had looked foward to a really relaxed evening; but she believed in doing what had to be done, even if tiresome, without delay, or at least only the delay of a cup of tea; and what had to be done now was to get rid of those kittens.

Janet knew very little about animals. She would never have been consciously cruel to one but she was almost totally ignorant of their habits and needs. They were not part of her world. Cows, sheep and the occasional horse she accepted as objects in a landscape. Dogs she disliked when she met them, as dirty, noisy and sometimes dangerous. They might keep burglars away but were almost as bad as burglars. Cats had their uses where mice were concerned, but in her view Maisie was not much more than an animated sort of mouse-trap. She remembered however, Mrs Binn's words about drowning kittens as soon as possible. Well, this was as soon as possible. After her tea she filled a bucket full of water and made her way to the shed. She found the business a more unpleasant job than she had anticipated. The little things were warm to her touch and struggled as she held them under the water. She had to keep telling herself that Mrs Binns had said they did not feel anything. An uncomfortable thought obtruded itself that Mrs Binns had drowned her lot sooner, but surely it didn't make all that difference. She had not expected either that Maisie would make such a fuss, in fact she hadn't thought about her at all. After the kittens had been disposed of she shut her up in the shed and closed the window. The cat was making a

91

loud, continuous noise. When she got back to her room she felt exhausted; really it had been quite a day.

Harriet had got up early the morning of that same day and had paid Maisie and the kittens a visit before she went to school. Already she thought they were looking more like real kittens and she decided that the black and white one was going to be the prettiest, she could see his little shirt-front quite clearly. She was enraptured. She happened to be late home from school that day, it was her piano lesson afternoon and then, after she had had her tea and done her prep, Margot wouldn't let her go out again. "But I'll get up early so as to see Maisie and the kittens before school. I mean to go and see them every morning."

Janet too was up early. She had noticed that her michaelmas daisies wanted staking — they had grown so while she was away, and the wind was getting up. She was interrupted by Harriet.

"I can't find the kittens," she said, "and Maisie's miaowing dreadfully. Have you got them here, Miss Cook? I know they're lovely but Maisie wants them back."

Janet Cook felt uncomfortably embarrassed and this made her speak brusquely.

"There aren't any kittens any longer. Cats have far too many, you know; they have to be got rid of."

Harriet stared at her, then: "What do you mean, 'got rid of', you don't mean *killed*, do you?" she asked in a whisper — the words were too dreadful to say aloud.

"Now," said Janet, the more sharply for an irrepressible, though she considered a quite unwarranted, sense of guilt, "don't be silly, when people don't want kittens, they always drown them, you know; they are much too little to feel anything."

Harriet, after a shocked silence, shouted loudly: "I hate you, you're a wicked woman!"

The ingrained red of Janet Cook's cheeks became

redder. "And you're a very rude little girl," she rejoined, but Harriet had fled.

She had to see Mrs Sanderson at once. "You've got a murderess in your house, Mrs Sanderson," she cried when she had found her, "you won't let her stay, will you?"

"Is it the kittens?" asked Letty apprehensively. Harriet answered with a flood of tears.

Oh dear! thought Letty, *Oh dear, dear, dear!* Aloud she said, "Don't cry so, darling, they were too young to know anything about it." But Harriet did not believe her, nor really did Letty herself.

"But Maisie, *poor* Maisie," Harriet sobbed, "she's calling and calling for them."

"She'll forget about it in a day or two," said Letty, this time with more conviction, "she really will, Harriet."

Harriet stopped sobbing in consternation. "But she oughtn't to forget," she cried, "I don't want her to forget!"

"Do you want her to go on being miserable, then?" asked Letty.

Harriet was silent. She did and she didn't — all she really knew she wanted, and that passionately, was to have the kittens alive again.

It was a miserable day. That evening Harriet said to Andrew: "Do kittens go to heaven?"

"I don't know," said Andrew.

Harriet sighed; if Andrew didn't know, no one would know, but on the other hand, if he didn't know one way or other, there was still a hope that they did.

CHAPTER EIGHT

THE IMPROVEMENT IN his job that Aubrey Stacey had hoped for after his move to the attic flat in the Lotus House had not materialized. It was indeed a relief to return to his peaceful rooms after the day's ordeal instead of the incessant noise and permanent smell of stale smoke of his old lodgings, but at school matters became even worse. He had been allotted an older class of mixed ability. The mixture was divided roughly into three groups — the aggressive, the apathetic and a minority who, with a possible GCE as a target, gravitated to the front of the classroom where they were just able to hear the teacher and, by ignoring what went on elsewhere, managed with difficulty to accomplish a little work.

A ringleader amongst the first group was an overweight black-browed girl called Marcia. She had quickly classified Aubrey as a creep and thenceforth as fair game. His subsequent mortification was systematically planned. There was first the straightforward crude "hubbub" ordeal to which each of the staff in turn were subjected as a matter of course. Aubrey, as Marcia expected, fell into the trap and responded by shouts of, "Silence, stop that row at once."

Silence immediately ensued but it was too complete, too sudden, and soon the tapping began — tap, tap, tap of ball-point pens on desks, and then of boxes and transistors, anything handy, gradually mounting to a crescendo and then dying down, only to start again after a pause. Next there was the veiled insult, the innuendo that must not be noticed in case worse should follow, and the provocative personalities:

"Oh, Mister, I like your shirt — look at Mister's shirt. Cool, isn't it?"

"Did your wife choose it for you?"

"You boob, he hasn't got a wife."

"Hasn't he? Well, now's your chance then, Tracey."

"Why hasn't he?"

"Oh, Mister, Pete's *bent* my book!" (Hilarious laughter).

"Mister, tell Marcia not to take off her cardigan, I can see her big boobs and it's distracting me."

"Yes, what is it, Doreen?"

"What's what, Mister?"

"You had your hand up."

'Oh, I was only combing my hair."

Or, again, there was the stonewalling ordeal, and in this the apathetic group would often join.

"But it's so *boring*, it doesn't *mean* anything. What the hell's the guy after?"

"It's like difficult to do this, Mister."

"Why should we anyways? My Mum, she never had to bother with this dope and she's done all right."

Lastly there was the absolute defiance — "Pass us a fag, mate," or a chair hurled across the room, a window broken deliberately.

After each failure to cope with one or other of these challenges, Aubrey sought escape from humiliation in dreams of his true vocation as a writer; after all, no creative genius could be expected to succeed as a hack teacher — look at the Brontës, look at D.H. Lawrence. He would get out his manuscript and sit with it before him, his pick-me-up at hand which he felt to be not

95

only a necessity but a just compensation for what he had to endure during the day. Often the whole evening would slip away in a vague pleasant trance which he excused to himself as a period of gestation. True inspiration could only occur at the right time, when the subconscious had done the preparatory work, so this period of relaxation was not at all a waste of time.

But as he filled and refilled the glass beside him, his musings over his plot and characters were apt to merge into bright fantasies. The six presentation copies of the finished book lay there on his table, together with the reviews, all highly appreciative, or he heard his brother calling him up on the phone, or better still, appearing at the Lotus House with a bottle of champagne under each arm to celebrate, or he was receiving the congratulations of his headmaster and the staff. Best of all he pictured his mother and father overcome with pride and pleasure. After such an evening he would put away his manuscript in a euphoric haze. Then would follow the deep oblivion of the night; and next morning a hangover and the grim reality of another school day. He sometimes thought of giving in his notice but shrank from the confession of failure; also his parents were not rich and he could not see himself living on the dole, having no taste for economy, and it would not be easy to find another job, for he could not hope for an enthusiastic recommendation. Anyway, would another teaching post be any better, there were worse places, he knew, and he lacked the confidence to launch out into fresh fields. No, he must keep on until his novel was finished.

But the autumn term brought some improvement. In the holidays he had had two weeks' holiday in Greece, where he had been intoxicated by colour and warmth. He was among friendly, civilized people, and the world of sordid savagery in south-east London seemed thousands of miles away, tiny, unreal and of no importance.

96

Although, on his return, this impression naturally faded, he felt the benefit in health and spirits. Surely things must be better this term, and so, at first, they were. Marcia and her chief cronies were themselves in sight of freedom, being due to leave at Christmas, and therefore less aggressive. Besides, baiting the same creep for so long became boring, like everything else. And then there was Hassan. He was a new boy, a Pakistani with a mobile intelligent face and the large appealing dark eyes of his race. Aubrey immediately became aware of those eyes fixed upon him in eager anticipation. Here was someone actually anxious to learn. He felt as if, parched with thirst, he had been offered a drink of water. He soon discovered that the boy was responsive and sensitive even to the poor material he was handing out to him.

When he had first started at Brook Comprehensive he had intended, as had been his custom, to include some carefully selected classics into his general syllabus, but this hope was quickly dispelled.

"My dear Stacey, we keep in touch with reality here. Teach them, if you can, to speak and write grammatically and to spell, that's your priority; they'll need that to get jobs. As for any reading, go easy — there's quite a useful anthology on the staffroom shelves — Salinger and that *Lord of the Flies* man, and Wynham."

"Poetry?" Aubrey had asked tentatively.

"No go, my dear chap, they won't take it, I'm afraid, though if you're keen you might try to squeeze in a contemporary now and again. There was a fellow I heard on the radio the other day, a description of a decaying fish, very lifelike I thought it — you a fisherman?"

"No."

"Well, you wouldn't appreciate it then. But something like that might appeal."

Now, however, Aubrey found himself longing to try out on this boy some of his favourites, and this became

97

compelling after he had had Hassan's first bit of written work. He had read the class a descriptive passage of D.H. Lawrence out of the staffroom anthology, about the Australian bush, and then told them to write what they remembered of it and what they liked or disliked about it — a routine exercise from which he expected little. Half the class would never attempt it, would not even have listened. "It doesn't mean anything anyway," "What right's he got to bother us!" The rest would vary in presentation but would be depressingly similar as to content. Then suddenly he came upon this:

"Words are magic things, sometimes they dance, sometimes they cry, sometimes they sing. Some are terrible, some take me travelling. This man's words make me feel alone, the only person left in the world, but I do not mind because I am changed into a magician by his words. I can do and see anything I wish."

Aubrey, staring at the round careful script, was silent upon his peak in Darien. His discovery filled him with excitement, almost with awe. From then on he taught for Hassan, waited in suspense for his response, contrived opportunities to see the boy alone that would appear accidental — excuses to retain him after class, or seemingly chance meetings out of school. He began to lend him books: poetry, Stevenson, Kipling, the short stories of Conrad; which the boy returned shyly, without much comment, but with such glowing looks of appreciation that expressed better than words that they had done their work. Aubrey experienced in all this the deepest satisfaction that life had yet offered him. He planned how he would continue to nourish Hassan's talent, how, as he grew older, Hassan would become a real friend as well as a pupil, yet would always keep that gratitude and admiration for himself that he now gave so innocently and openly. Too openly, too innocently, for after a time things began to go wrong.

Aubrey had been aware that he must be cautious about the relationship, but he was not conscious of how his face lit up whenever he spoke to the boy, nor that Hassan's response had been noted as beyond even that expected by the despised and ridiculed "snobs" in the front row. Hassan became all of a sudden withdrawn and silent during lessons and avoided all other possible encounters. Then one day, after the others had all gone, he did return to the classroom with Aubrey's copy of "The Ancient Mariner", which he hastily thrust at him with a quick glance over his shoulder and round the room.

"Thank you, sir," he half whispered, "but do not lend me any more just now, please — I am too busy." He was gone before Aubrey could detain him and as he started up to try and do so he thought he saw a face pressed against the window.

The next morning as he came into the room, there was a sudden unnatural hush. He opened his desk to get out his books and there, lying on the top of them, was a large bold drawing executed with a crude vigour in black and red. It was an obscene picture of himself and Hassan and beneath was scrawled "Mr Stacey is a bent." The drawing gave Aubrey an almost physical sensation of a violent blow between the eyes. It was probably for only a second or two that he gazed at it behind the shelter of the desk lid, though it seemed an age. Then he became conscious of the air of suppressed excitement in the classroom and with a tremendous effort he controlled his rage and disgust. Hassan . . . he must think of Hassan, and force himself to carry on the lesson as usual. Aware of rows of eyes fixed upon him in expectation, aware, alas, though how he did not know for he did not look at him, of the boy crouching down over his books, he heard himself saying quietly, "Get out your exercises and take down a dictation." Mechanically he started reading out the passage — "Think of this sentence," he ordered him-

99

self, "now, the next and the next — now collect the books, now write up the difficult words on the board, now ask for their meanings — soon the bell will go and the lesson will be over. Nothing exists for you except the next necessary action."

"Not so hot after all," said Doreen at the end of the morning. "Looks as if old Creep Stacey's got no bloody eye for art."

"Oh, fuck it," said Marcia.

"Watcher doin' tonight? Goin' home?"

"You must be kidding, my Mum's got her new bloke there, or she'll be out with him and not back till morning."

"Where you goin' then?"

"What bloody business is it of yours?" said Marcia, pushing her way through the crowd.

"What the hell's got her?" asked Tracey.

"*She* won't be home till the morning either, if I know her," said Doreen.

"She got a Dad?" enquired one of the others. "My Dad'd bloody well murder me if I didn't show up."

"Never had none as far as I know," said Doreen.

Luckily it was a Friday, the day when the afternoon was supposed to be given over to organized games and crafts, so Aubrey was free. He had intended a visit to the British Museum to look up some fresh data on the lately neglected hero of his novel, but now his one wish was to get drunk as soon and as thoroughly as possible. He reached home, unaware of the journey or of anything but the goal ahead, but before he could start on his drinking bout there was one thing that had to be done. He took out of his pocket the crushed ball of paper that was Marcia's drawing. This must be destroyed at once. In feeling for some matches in another pocket to set it on fire, he came across the little volume of Coleridge where he had thrust it on the previous day, and recalled how he had looked

100

forward to sharing its glory with Hassan. A wave of love and loss swept over him and he threw the book across the room. By late afternoon he was lying on his bed in the desired state.

Something wonderful had happened to Harriet that day at school. It wasn't that Miss Johnson had said "good" after her piano lesson which made her feel powerful and good, (she had been learning nearly a year now and Miss Johnson not infrequently praised her), but this time she had added; "I think you already manage the little Mozart piece almost well enough to be able to play it at the end of term Christmas concert."

"Do you mean the big one when everyone comes?" asked Harriet incredulously. She had heard this event talked about with awe.

"Yes, would you like that?" asked Miss Johnson.

"I don't know," said Harriet, "I think I *would*. Mothers and fathers come, don't they?"

"Oh yes," said Miss Johnson, "especially the ones whose children are playing, we keep special seats in front for them. It's great fun. Now, just run through the sonatina again."

This time the notes seemed to play themselves, Harriet's fingers didn't have to find them on the keyboard at all. She loved this piece, the little twinkles that Mozart had put in here and there always reminded her of the way the stars twinkled and flashed at her through her window on clear nights.

When she had finished Miss Johnson said "That is really very nice indeed, Harriet, you can tell your mother now that you will certainly be playing at the concert. Of course she'll get a proper invitation soon."

At the end of the afternoon Harriet ran all the way home. She was early. Mrs Sanderson let her in but was on the point of going out to visit a friend, Andrew was not at home and Margot too was not yet back, and there was no sound from the basement either; not that Harriet would have felt like telling Miss Cook her great news, the murder of the kittens was too recent a tragedy. The whole big house seemed empty and silent. Well, there was always the doll's house family. She knew she wasn't supposed to go into Mrs Sanderson's room except on Saturdays but now she had to. Harriet Royce, alias Wilhelmina Rose, *must* tell her mother and father she was playing in the school concert. They clapped their hands for joy. Harriet thought she had better not stay long with them in case Mrs Sanderson came back and found her there and was cross. She gave every room in the little Lotus House a loving happy glance before she shut it up, and seeing the grandfather on his bed upstairs made her wonder if perhaps the big house wasn't quite empty after all, for Mr Stacey might be at home and she could tell her news to him. She had never been up to the attic floor before but the need to communicate was too great for shyness.

When she reached the top landing she thought she heard a noise coming from the back room and she knocked on the door. No one answered so she opened the door and looked in. The room smelt very queer. She took a step inside and saw that Mr Stacey *was* there. He was lying on his bed with his eyes shut. This did not surprise her for, although part of her knew quite well that he was not the doll's house grandfather on his bed in the top room of the little house, any more than Miss Cook was 'Cooksie' in the kitchen; yet as she had felt a compelling need to identify the doll's house parents with her own parents, and their dolly daughter with herself, the others had to follow suit: so it seemed somehow natural for the top-floor gentleman to be on his bed in the day time. And now, disturbed by her knocking and entry, Aubrey opened his eyes and saw a girl in a school uniform

102

standing inside his room and gazing at him, and all at once the rage and disgust he had been suppressing for so long took over.

He stretched out his hand and beckoned to Harriet. "Come over here," he whispered. The whisper sounded hoarse and strange and his hand was trembling. This, and the fact that he did not ask her what she wanted but seemed to have been waiting for her, frightened Harriet, she did not know why. But all the same his eyes were so compelling that she took a step or two towards him.

Man and child both stared at each other as if mesmerized. It had been a grey, sultry day of low cloud, but now the setting sun suddenly blazed out, and threw the shadow of the old nursery bars across the white coverlet of Aubrey's bed — his gaze deflected on them for a minute, and at once, as if released, Harriet called out, "No, no!" Aubrey's arm dropped. "Go away," he shouted, "go away at once," and Harriet turned and went.

After she had gone Aubrey staggered over to his basin and was very sick, then he lay down again and fell into a series of half-waking nightmares. He was always conscious of being in his room and lying on his bed, but from a corner of the room came the sound of his own voice chanting relentlessly and monotonously the *Rime of the Ancient Mariner*. Presently there seemed to be a huge white bird flying round and round the ceiling and beating against the window, trying to escape. He knew at once it was the albatross and that soon he would be forced to kill it. More horrible still, as it flew it turned a child's face towards him — Hassan's, then Harriet's as she had looked at him from the door — but then, before he had even fired the inescapable shot, the body of the bird began to disintegrate and dissolve and the room was full of white feathers, cold feathers, snowflakes falling upon his bed and heaping themselves upon him. And now the

103

voice from the corner changed to his mother's reading aloud from Hans Andersen. "In the midst of the empty endless hall of snow was a frozen lake and in the centre of this lake sat the Snow Queen when she was at home. Little Kay was quite blue with cold and his heart was already a lump of ice."

This can't be a dream, thought Aubrey, *or I could not remember the words*, yet he knew that it was his mother who was the Ice Queen and he was little Kay. He felt very cold — he was lying uncovered and it was now night and the room was full of a white light, so that the shadow of the nursery bars still showed. He pulled the bedclothes over himself and another verse of Coleridge's mighty poem quoted itself to him:

"The moving moon went up the sky and nowhere did abide,

Softly she was going up and a star or two beside."
Warmth began to steal over him and he drowsed off once more and again a voice was speaking. This time it was Mrs Sanderson showing him the room. "This was the old night nursery. I have slept here many a time long ago — it still seems to me the safest place in the world."

After this he awoke thoroughly, got up and undressed and washed. The little volume of Coleridge lay on the floor in the corner where he had tossed it. He picked it up and replaced it carefully on his shelves. Then, knowing himself for the first time capable of both crime and redemption, he lay down and slept, this time deeply and dreamlessly, till late morning.

CHAPTER NINE

ON THE MORNING of the concert, Harriet woke to see an unclouded square of pale wintry blue through her window. She was glad, not that it mattered all that much for a concert if the sun were shining, but grey skies and rain would not have felt right. She was too excited to eat her breakfast. Andrew, who was anxious over the outcome of an experiment, had gone off early to his laboratory and Margot was hastily looking over her post. She always felt slightly aggrieved when Andrew left the house first and she had everything to see to, including getting Harriet off for school.

"What's the matter with you?" she said, becoming aware of the untouched food. "You've just messed about with your egg — I hate waste."

"It's because of the concert," said Harriet.

"Oh, I'd forgotten, it's today, is it?"

"But you're coming?" said Harriet, suddenly consumed with anxiety.

"Yes, of course," said Margot, "what time is it?"

The time was engraved on Harriet's heart, it was also on the invitation card which she had proudly brought home some time ago and which now lay among the pile of papers which Margot kept in a fruit bowl on her desk, but she was glad her mother had asked so that she could tell her once again. "It begins at half-past two and performers' parents are having the first two rows kept for them."

"What a godless hour," said Margot. "Well, if you won't eat a proper breakfast you won't, I suppose, so hurry up now and be off."

"You won't be late?" Harriet couldn't help asking.

"Don't fuss, I'm not Andrew," said Margot.

During that morning she had a phone call from a young sculptor, Crispin Keylock, whose work they were showing at her shop.

"It's awfully short notice but could you possibly lunch with me today? I'm feeling good this morning — I've just finished a presentation portrait bust and want to celebrate, and I'm off tomorrow to France, which makes too long a gap before I see you again."

Margot hesitated. "That would be lovely, but I've got to be at my daughter's school concert by 2.30," she said.

"How ghastly for you, but how admirable. We'll make it early then, shall we? I'll fetch you at noon." The lunch *was* early but it was also absorbing and delightful, and when Margot thought to look at her watch it was already nearly 3 o'clock.

"You should have reminded me," she said.

"You could hardly expect that, I'm human after all," he replied, "and now, as I suppose you've got the afternoon off, what about that new film at the Curzon?"

While watching the film Margot managed to stifle any compunction as to the concert, but when she was driving home afterwards she felt the need to justify herself. "She'll soon get over it. I'll take her out at the weekend if I'm free, anyway she may even have been relieved, playing in front of one's family Andrew always said is an ordeal worse than playing to strangers, she's probably done much better without me."

Harriet had spent the morning in a daze but it did not seem to matter, for allowances were made. She played

106

her piece once through again to Miss Johnson, who said it went very well. At dinner time she found she was suddenly very hungry. Then there was an interminable period of doing nothing in particular, until at last it was time to watch for the parents and friends to arrive.

"Oh, there's Mummy and Dad," called out Susan Phillips, who was playing a recorder solo just before Harriet. Then more and more mums and dads arrived and were hailed with joy.

"My mother is more pretty and wonderful than any of them," said Harriet to herself. "When she comes everyone will look at her, they always do. Miss Johnson said I played well this morning and I shall play better this afternoon and everyone will clap me and Mummy will clap too."

Presently she began to be anxious, the front rows of reserved seats were filling up fast. They all had little tickets on them and Harriet knew where Margot's seat was, towards the centre of the second row. Soon it was the only empty one and she felt, inside her, something ticking away very quickly. Then Miss Johnson herded them all together into the little classroom at the back of the big hall and the concert began. There was Barbara and Tessa's duet, and next Susan's solo, and then it was Harriet's turn. As she crossed the stage to the piano she could see that there was still one empty seat where her mother should have been. She sat down and began to play, but her fingers felt like heavy lumps and she couldn't see the music properly, everything was blurred. She hadn't really needed the music either, because she could play the piece perfectly well without, but now she couldn't remember it at all. She stumbled on to the end and the audience clapped kindly and loudly, though she did not hear them.

"Why, Harriet," said Miss Johnson, "you must learn not to give way to stage fright so badly as that!" and then, looking at her more closely, she added: "Never mind, it was a pity, but it can't be helped now."

Harriet said nothing. No one saw her slip away, they were all too busy. She did not ask for leave to go home and no one stopped her. When she got there she found Andrew in the sitting-room, immersed and frowning over his papers.

"Where's Margot?" said Harriet. Although when she had been playing she had had to blink and blink away her tears, now she did not want to cry any more.

"Hasn't come home yet," said Andrew, not looking up, "and look here, be a good Harriet and don't bother just now, will you?"

She went through the little kitchen that led to the landing. By the kitchen door Margot, with her usual efficiency, had put up a rack to hold all the household tools. Harriet took the hammer from its place and went downstairs again. Presently Mrs Sanderson, coming in from a visit, saw that her bedroom door was open and heard an odd sound of splintering wood.

Burglars, she thought at once, and went intrepidly to confront them. What she saw was Harriet hacking Selina's doll's house to pieces.

"Harriet!" she shouted.

Harriet dropped the hammer in the middle of the wreckage and turned to face her.

"It's the bomb!" she cried in a curious shrill voice, "it's the bomb and it's killed them all dead!" Then she burst into sobs and rushed past Letty out of the room.

Aubrey Stacey was coming home and just approaching the gate when he saw Harriet running towards him. On seeing him, she swerved away off the path into the road straight in front of an oncoming tradesman's van. The van pulled up with a screech of brakes but it had caught the child, who fell backwards against the curb. Aubrey ran forward as the driver of the van was getting out. He looked very pale.

"You saw it, sir," he said, "I hadn't a chance of missing her."

"Yes," said Aubrey, "it wasn't your fault."

"What happened to the other child?" asked the man.

"There wasn't another child that I could see," said Aubrey.

The man looked puzzled. "I saw her," he said, "she caught at this one to pull her back – if it hadn't been for her, I'd have gone right over her."

"Well, this isn't the time to argue," said Aubrey kneeling down by Harriet. "She's breathing all right, stay here. I must go and phone for a doctor and an ambulance," and he rushed into the house.

Mrs Sanderson was still standing in her room gazing at the wreck of the doll's house when she heard Aubrey calling for her. After that it was all hurry and confusion, phone calls and interviews with the doctor and the police. Aubrey bore witness to the fact that the van driver was not to blame. He stuck to his story of another little girl but she was never traced. Harriet lay in a coma at the hospital. She had a broken leg but that was not serious, the doctor, however, could not yet pronounce on the extent of injury to her head.

At the Lotus House where she had been so unobtrusive, so shadowy a little presence, she was now inescapably important. All, in various degrees felt guilty, though each kept this to themselves. Letty blamed herself for shirking the implications of those overheard doll's house conversations; could she have helped without appearing interfering in what was not her business? She did not know, but she had not tried; and how could she have not followed a desperate sobbing child out of the house! Aubrey Stacey believed that Harriet, whom he had scarcely seen since she had visited his room, had swerved into the road to avoid him. Janet Cook unwillingly recalled the scene in the garden about the kittens. *I suppose it wouldn't have hurt to have kept one*, she thought. Andrew cursed himself for not having remembered that it had been the day of the concert and that Harriet ought not have have been coming home at that hour, nor Margot to have been at work, and why did he have to tell the child to go away — she was never any real nuisance.

But what Margot felt was the absence of feeling. She had refused to discuss the concert with Andrew. "I had an expected engagement crop up," she said, "and when it was over it was too late."

Andrew, taking it for granted that it was a business matter she could not have avoided, or thought she could not, refrained from pressing her or reproaching her in any way. To judge others was almost pathologically alien to him; besides he imagined with sympathy that she must be remorselessly judging herself. They drove to the hospital every day and sat by Harriet for a short while. A week after the accident there was little or no change; she sometimes moaned and clutched her hands but did not open her eyes or show any consciousness of their presence. One day as they got up to go, Margot saw Andrew lean over and very gently put back a strand of the straight heavy hair from the child's forehead. A sudden strange pang of envy consumed her. "He knows how to love, but I don't, I never have."

During that troubled week everyone concerned knew a part, but not the whole truth about the accident. Miss Johnson, who assumed it had happened on the way back from the school, believed that upset by the fiasco of her performing at the concert, the child had been terribly heedless of the traffic. Aubrey, unaware of why she was rushing from the house, rightly guessed she had dashed into the road to avoid him, though he was wrong in her reasons for so doing — she would have done so whoever it had been.

110

Miss Cook's theory was that Harriet must have been escaping from an attack by one of those dreadful estate boys. Andrew and Margot both suspected that her mother's failure to turn up at the concert was somehow responsible, but they were ignorant as to the destruction of the doll's house. Letty, only too conscious of this, was anxious to keep it secret. Harriet's bomb had done its work thoroughly: there was no possibility of repair. Letty found a few little pots and pans and two bent fireplaces among the debris. The bodies of Mr and Mrs Golightly Royce, the grandfather and Cooksie looked as if they had been stamped upon: only Wilhelmina Rose Harriet had escaped all injury. She was found under a chair where she had fallen clear of the house. Letty had picked her up and laid her away in her handkerchief drawer. She had then consigned the wreckage to the dustbin sack, she could not bear to look at it. She trusted that Dian with her habitual lack of interest in objects above the floor level, would not comment on the doll's house's disappearance. Ignorant on her part of the fiasco of the concert, she wondered continually what could have caused this whole disastrous crisis.

In the days that followed she felt wretchedly depressed. Harriet's bomb seemed to have shattered not only the doll's house but much else. It was time to stop playing Happy Families, she thought, and to put away the useless cards. The beloved image of the Lotus House was itself menaced, it was after all no more now than a lodging for five unhappy people — no, six counting herself. The darker symbolism of its name struck her for the first time — the Lotus House — the house of delusive dreams. Were all the memories she had cherished only the bitter-sweet myth of childhood? *Stop telling your stories, Selina, stop, stop. Through what struggles and suffering may you and all your family have had to pass to the final defeat. "We'll be coming back," you said, but you never came back.*

111

She was alone in her sitting-room; the short winter daylight was fading and the fire had sunk to a dull glow, but she did not move, but sat on in the darkness. At last she got up to put on the light. "The past is gone now beyond recall," she said, speaking aloud as if addressing the great empty room. But the dark bulk of the house she felt all around her seemed to answer defiantly, "Yet the past is here now, beyond oblivion." As she drew the long curtains, a child's laugh sounded faintly from the dark garden. *The children are playing late on the estate,* she thought, *their mothers let them stay out in the cold and dark at all hours nowadays.*

Ten days after the accident Harriet opened her eyes for the first time. There was no one at hand but a nurse, who hearing a slight movement bent at once over the bed. Harriet was staring into space with an unmistakable look of horror, she murmured something almost indistinguishable and shut her eyes again.

"She spoke, you say — did you hear what she said?" asked the doctor.

"I'm not sure," said the nurse, "but it sounded like: 'I've killed them all dead'."

"A nightmare," said the doctor, "those wretched TV films all about murders, and children *will* watch them. We must get her mother here at once. Meanwhile, stop with her, nurse, hold her hand and talk to her, anything soothing that comes into your head."

It was lucky that this particular nurse had younger brothers and sisters and possessed a fund of nursery rhymes and songs, for she had gone through many before Margot arrived.

"Doctor says, hold her hand and comfort her by repeating anything she used to hear from you when she was a baby, but you'll know what is best to do better than I can tell you, Mrs Royce."

Margot took the small limp hand in hers but she

experienced nothing but the repulsion that any illness always produced in her and she could not think of anything at all to say. The nurse, passing and repassing, glanced at her in surprise and Margot, always acutely aware of others' reactions towards herself, felt both resentful and embarrassed.

Yet her touch seemed to reach through to Harriet after a little while, for she opened her eyes again and this time, seeing her mother sitting by her, she said quite clearly with a look of intense joy and relief, "Oh, I thought I had killed you dead."

"Darling, what nonsense," said Margot, "you've been having a horrid dream."

Then she drifted off once more, but presently she spoke again. "Where am I?" she asked.

"You're in hospital, there was an accident, you got knocked down by a van, but you'll soon be well again now, so don't worry and don't have any more silly dreams." Harriet gave her mother a long pleased look and then with a small sigh of contentment she dropped off into a natural sleep.

Andrew came in later and she woke again.

"I can't move my leg," Harriet confided to him in a whisper. She seemed puzzled rather than alarmed.

"You've broken it," said Andrew cheerfully. "Not to worry, legs mend again quite easily, especially when they are young ones."

But Harriet frowned. Something seemed to be troubling her again.

"I broke all their legs," she whispered. "I know it wasn't really you and Margot now, but I broke everything."

"Well, I shouldn't worry about that," said Andrew firmly. "She seems still to be bothered with bad dreams," he told the nurse.

"I expect it's the leg paining her, but she's doing fine.

Doctor's pleased with her."

"Harriet wants to see you, Mrs Sanderson," said Margot a few days later, "she seems to have something on her mind about your doll's house. We think it's from a nightmare she had when she was coming round from the coma. Do you think you could fit in a visit soon, it would be so kind?"

"Of course," said Letty, "I was only waiting till you thought it advisable for visitors other than you and Mr Royce."

Before leaving for the hospital, Letty took Wilhelmina Rose Harriet out of her drawer and slipped her into her bag.

"I remember properly now," said Harriet as soon as the nurse had left them alone together. "I didn't at first. I smashed the little house as well as the people. I'm so sorry." Tears began to roll down her cheeks. "Is *everyone* killed?"

"Not everyone," said Letty. She fished in her bag and brought out Wilhelmina Rose Harriet and laid her on the bed. Harriet clutched her with both hands but the tears came faster than ever.

"Why, whatever is the matter?" said Nurse Hutchinson appearing again. "We never cry, not even when our leg hurts." She turned a reproachful eye on poor Letty. "We're *such* a good girl *always*." She mopped away the tears. "I think she's had enough of visitors for today," she said rather severely.

Letty kissed Harriet's damp cheeks and went away as she was told but, in spite of the nurse, she suspected that those tears were not a bad thing.

"Where did that funny little doll come from?" asked Margot that same evening.

"Mrs Sanderson brought her," said Harriet.

"I should have thought she would have suspected you were too old to play with dolls," said Margot.

114

"I shan't play with her," said Harriet.

"Well, she'll do as a mascot, I suppose," said Margot.

"What's a mascot?" enquired Harriet the next day of her never-failing encyclopaedia.

"Something to bring you good luck," said Andrew.

Harriet smiled.

A time came when the doctor said "I think you can look forward to having Harriet at home soon, Mrs Royce. Of course she'll need nursing and careful treatment for some time yet, but we don't want to hospitalize her longer than necessary. She could come to you in about another week, I should think."

Margot responded after a very slight hesitation and not with quite the eagerness he had expected, but he thought her a delightful woman and sensible too, quite free from that neurotic fussiness he often met with in mothers.

"Andrew," said Margot that evening, "the doctor says Harriet can leave the hospital next week."

"Really!" exclaimed Andrew, "That's good."

"I suppose she'd better go to the guest-room."

"Of course, her own's much too small."

"She'll need a lot of care for some time," he said.

"Well, you'll be able to get leave, I'm sure," said Andrew, "you're too valuable for them to make any fuss, especially in these circumstances."

There was a silence, then Margot said, "It's no use, Andrew, I can't face it, I'm the world's worst nurse, I loathe it and it simply wouldn't work. She'd do better in a convalescent home somewhere."

This time it was Andrew's turn to be silent.

"I know what you're thinking," burst out Margot at last, "that I ought to have gone to that bloody concert and that at least now I ought to be able to look after my own child, but how was I to know she'd take it like that, and am I responsible for that van being there just at that moment?"

115

"You've never let yourself realize how she adores you," said Andrew.

"Yes, I have," exclaimed Margot, "and it always exasperates me, it did with Dick, too, and with others. Oh, Andrew," and suddenly she sounded humble and defenceless, "the truth is I don't know how to love or be loved."

Andrew got up and came over to her. He disliked emotional scenes and was certainly not used to them from Margot, and words seemed to him useless. He suspected that what she said was true and yet he had never liked her so much before. He put an arm round her and pressed her gently to him. After a while as they stood there he said "Harriet must come home here, you know that really, don't you? We'll manage all right somehow, you'll see."

But he did not quite see until astonishingly Miss Cook came to their rescue. She was astonished herself. She had been upset of course by the accident, well, that was natural, a child under the same roof, anyone would be. But unwarrantably, yes, she told herself, quite unwarrantably, she was still haunted by her last encounter with Harriet which would not have bothered her at all, she felt, had it not been for the accident, but there it was. Dian had told her that Harriet was coming home soon.

"Mrs Royce, she wanted to know if I could spare her some extra time; well, I'm that sorry but I can't, it would mean letting down my other ladies, see — not used to having the child on her hands all day and don't look forward to it, I can tell you."

Janet Cook thought about this for some time. She had had very little experience of children but she supposed she could help look after a little girl as well as anyone else if she gave her mind to it. So one afternoon that week Andrew answered a knock on the door and found Miss Cook on the threshold. He ushered her into the sitting-room; she had never been there before and looked around with interest.

Striking, she thought, *but not at all pretty — that picture, just squares of black and red, not worth framing, I'd say, and that huge silver lamp hanging on a chain like something out of a church, not proper in a room.* And then she saw Crispin Keylock's carved elongated female nude and decided she did not like the room at all. The thought darted into her mind, rather shocking her, that it, like Doris' lounge, might be improved by some of Luke's matchboxes.

"What can I do for you, Miss Cook?" enquired Andrew politely, for she had been so busy looking round that she had not spoken yet.

"Well, it's like this, Dr Royce," she said, "I hear that little Harriet is coming home soon, and if Mrs Royce wants a hand with looking after her, amusing her and so forth, and I've done a bit of nursing too in my time, I'd be glad to help. Neighbours should be neighbourly, you know." Could this be her mother's daughter speaking thus? Most unlikely, but so it was, and when all was said and done really it was those five. little drowned kitten corpses that were responsible.

Miss Cook's offer was gratefully accepted and Letty also promised help, so Margot was able to keep her job going and Harriet, in due course, came home.

CHAPTER TEN

AT FIRST ALL went well. Harriet was happier now than at any period she could remember. She was a different Harriet, an important person, and yet at the same time someone for whom nothing was important. Time no longer mattered, nor lessons, nor what she said or what she didn't say. The past didn't matter, in fact she didn't seem to remember the events that led up to her accident at all clearly — it was like a bad dream, though it seemed somehow important to keep the little doll's house girl within reach. People sent this Harriet "Get Well" cards, which stood in a row on the mantelpiece opposite the spare-room bed in which she lay in splendour and gazed at them. There was one from Mrs Campbell and Lucy and Rebecca, and one from Squinty and one from Miss Johnson, and a large beautiful one of birds and flowers and rabbits signed by all her class, including Ben, in his big bold hand. Then there were presents, chocolates from Mr Stacey, a manicure set from Dian which gave her great satisfaction, it was the first really grown-up present she had ever had. Miss Cook brought her a pink geranium in a pot and Andrew a jigsaw called "Farmyard Friends". Mrs Sanderson read stories to her and Miss Cook played games with her. Letty had wondered how Harriet would receive the ministrations of a murderess, but the drowning of the kittens also was now part of the bad dream;

besides Harriet, who heard the Bible read at school assembly and sometimes listened, remembered that Jesus had said God loves sparrows, and if He loved them, they must go to Heaven, and if sparrows, surely kittens, where presumably they get on well together. Also, because she was now an important person, Maisie was allowed to stay on her bed where, with the unerring instinct of a cat for comfort, she had located Harriet the day after she had returned from hospital, and Maisie was obviously now thoroughly contented and prosperous. Best of all, her mother spent the last waking hours of every day with Harriet. These periods however, were an increasing strain on Margot. She felt both inadequate and bored.

"How can any adult communicate with children? We live in different worlds," and she marvelled irritably at the way others seemed to bridge this gap.

"How have you been today, darling? How is the leg feeling?"

"Better, thank you." Then, what else was there to say? She fell back upon continuing the stories that Mrs Sanderson had been reading. Like everything else about Margot, her voice was attractive, low and clear, but she read aloud to Harriet badly, partly because she was not in the least interested in what she was reading, often indeed thinking her own thoughts simultaneously, and partly, because as if by doing so she could shorten the hour, she read very fast. But none of this mattered to Harriet, she knew Mrs Sanderson would read it all over again the next day. She was quite content to lie there and look at her mother and listen to the sound of her voice. But sometimes she sensed the impatience behind the reading and, thinking Margot was tired after her day's work, she would pretend to be asleep. Her mother would shut the book and go quietly away. "She doesn't kiss me goodnight because she's afraid of waking me, and when I'm awake she doesn't because we don't, but when I'm fast asleep she does."

119

But this halcyon period came to an end and before the geranium flower had withered or the "Get Well" cards had begun to curl at the edges, the indulgent reactions to "our little invalid", as Miss Cook always called her, showed signs of strain. By the time that Harriet was well enough to be dressed and move around with the aid of crutches, the atmosphere had changed. She had reached that stage of convalesence which is apt to be more trying than actual illness.

What a pity we are not characters in the kind of book I was given to read by my aunts long ago, thought Letty Sanderson, 'What Katy did' *and* 'The Daisy Chain', *for instance. Then Harriet would be the little Angel in the House and all of us would be ennobled by her misfortune.* But it wasn't like that for, with returning health, Harriet felt frustrated and fretful and actually her leg hurt her more now she was trying to use it. At the same time the patience of the grown-ups was becoming frayed. Miss Cook caught her cheating at Ludo one afternoon and she could not explain that it was because she felt too tired to finish the game.

"I don't play with little girls who cheat," said Janet Cook.

Harriet would not say she was sorry, so Janet stumped away downstairs. She was sometimes left to herself now for what seemed a long time — while she was in bed the hours had melted into one another, for she had slept so much.

"Now you can be in the sitting-room, Harriet, you can look at TV again — isn't that nice?"

But she didn't want to, she didn't want to do anything that she could do, only the things she couldn't do. She tried playing the piano one day but it had turned into an enemy. Andrew found her crouched over it in tears.

"It hates me, it won't do a thing I want," she sobbed.

"It's too soon, Harriet, it's made your head bad, you

120

mustn't try yet a while, promise."

And Maisie was banished from the flat. "I can't have that cat about any longer," said Margot, "she leaves her hairs all over the place and she's clawed the chairs."

Margot felt she needed a holiday badly. The Christmas break had been ruined by Harriet's accident. Now spring was in the air, always a time of restlessness. Crispin Keylock, whom she had been seeing fairly frequently, had suggested that she and Andrew might join him and his wife for two weeks trip up the Nile in April. She was attracted to the idea for it was less ordinary than Spain or Italy or Greece, where everybody went nowadays. Crispin's wife, whom she had met once or twice, had seemed an unassuming little creature, unlikely to be a nuisance to Andrew. Had Harriet been quite well there would have been no problems. Mrs Campbell ran a holiday camp at Easter and in the summer in some suitable country or seaside resort where Queensmead's or other parents could park their young, but the child was still suffering from headaches and her leg was not yet fully serviceable.

"You go," said Andrew, "I'll take some leave at home and look after the infant. I'm not all that keen on Egypt, I prefer a cold climate."

"Oh no," exclaimed Margot, though eagerly, "I can't let you do that."

"Nonsense, I'm not under your orders, my girl."

"Crispin will be disappointed if you don't come."

"You know he won't give a damn — come to think of it, I'm not sure I'd care for his company for two whole weeks."

"Why, don't you like him?" asked Margot curiously.

"I don't think he's a serious artist."

It wasn't the answer she had expected.

"What *do* you mean? His sculptures fetch very good prices."

"I dare say."

121

"Anyway, you're not qualified to judge."

"True enough. It doesn't matter anyway. You go and do your Cleopatra stuff and enjoy yourself, don't worry about me."

"You won't worry about *me*, I suppose," said Margot slowly, "I might have an affair with Crispin."

"Go ahead then," said Andrew, "God knows there's no value in our relationship, or any, that isn't free." He paused and then added, as if making a discovery —

"Come to think of it, God does know — of course that's why Adam had to fall."

"What *are* you talking about?" said Margot crossly, "Don't pretend you believe in God."

Andrew laughed. "Now I *have* shocked you!" He turned round on the piano stool upon which he was sitting and struck some bars of the Bach fugue that happened to be on the stand. Margot interrupted him.

"You never take me seriously. Why can't you answer me?"

"Don't I?" said Andrew, "I'm sorry, I meant this for an answer."

But Margot then and there decided that she certainly would go on the cruise and also amuse herself with Crispin if she felt like it. She needed a complete relaxation after all the strain of Harriet's illness.

One of Margot's charms was that she always looked so fresh with a crisp elegance that yet managed to seem perfectly natural. Letty Sanderson, coming in one morning from the garden where she had been picking the March daffodils, saw her standing in the hall with a letter which she had just taken from the postman and was obviously intent on reading immediately. She was wearing a pink and grey striped dress of some soft woollen material with a wide skirt gathered in at the waist by a matching pink belt, and she had a string of pale corals wound several times round her neck. The spring sunlight caught at the gold of the clasp and the buckle of the belt and at her shining hair. Letty found herself wishing she could keep her there, standing beside the curving white staircase beneath the graceful arch of the Lotus House hall. But then she looked up — her lovely eyes were sparkling and she was smiling to herself before she saw Letty, and though all she said then was a conventional greeting, it sounded like poetry.

"Really," said Letty to herself, "she's too delicious. How difficult life must be for her."

The letter Margot had been reading was from Crispin Keylock, giving details of the cruise and expressing extreme delight in the prospect of her company. She had been conscious lately of a longing to bask once again in the warmth and excitement of admiration and desire, not of course of the grovelling kind, but there was an undoubted austerity in living with Andrew. She was certainly due for a change.

When Harriet heard that her mother was going away and far away too, she was curiously upset, for although she saw little of her, she was yet the pivot upon which her world turned.

"Andrew will look after you," she was told.

"But what shall we do?" she asked Andrew disconsolately on the first evening after Margot's departure.

"Listen to things and go to places," he said, an answer which filled her with both curiosity and apprehension.

"What things and what places?" she asked.

"Wait and see," said Andrew, "I don't like talking while I'm eating" — they were at supper — "but we can begin now." He put on a record of Vivaldi which made a cheerful noise until they had finished.

"That low-down part that goes on and on the same is like Margot reading aloud," remarked Harriet thoughtfully.

Andrew laughed. "She wouldn't thank you for that," he

said, "but it's true enough."

Harriet looked shocked. "Oh, I didn't mean it wasn't nice," she said.

"It's nice in this bit of music, but it's not a nice way to read aloud. Don't think it's a crime to admit that Margot can't do everything perfectly or even very well. Music can be perfect, people can't."

Harriet frowned in the effort to absorb this.

"But it's people who make the music, that's funny!" Andrew looked at her appreciatively. "You're right, it's divinely funny. Actually there's a lot of funniness around, and don't forget your mother's part of it."

"*Is* she?" said Harriet frowning even harder.

In the days that followed Andrew quite often took her out somewhere in the car. Sometimes they even went as far as the sea. Once they went to a lunch-time concert in London and ate sandwiches afterards in St James' Park and fed the ducks. Except that he made her go to bed early and wash properly and do her exercises, Andrew treated Harriet as an equal, which was a new experience. She had never before felt herself the equal of anyone except perhaps Squinty. She did not always understand all the words he used nor exactly what he meant, but this did not matter. She had moved back to her own little bedroom now and she would lie and look up at her sky and think about what they had done and talked about during the day.

Sometimes in the evenings Andrew would say "Let's be silly," and they were — very silly. Letty Sanderson used to hear them laughing. She remarked on it once when she took a note up to Andrew which had been left for him.

"I like to hear it," she said. "In the old days there always seemed to be laughter about this house."

"I used to hear people laughing," said Harriet unex-

124

pectedly, "when I was in the guest-room before I could get up."

"You must have been dreaming," said Andrew.

"Yes," agreed Harriet, "I was rather mixed up but it was nice."

Meanwhile Margot was not feeling at all like laughing. She had supposed that the East would hold enchantment, the days beguiling her with exotic sights, sounds and scents, the velvet nights full of huge stars. Instead she found days of dust and dirt, and nights full of huge mosquitoes. The boat, boarded at Cairo, was the first disappointment. It was uncomfortably old-fashioned, no air-conditioning, verging on tawdriness, undeniably smelly and the few single cabins were the least supportable. Hers, she discovered, was the noisiest and had a broken fan, but it took Margot only one day to subjugate a fellow single-cabin passenger. This was a middle-aged, kind, dehydrated American lady, very vulnerable to charm.

"My little girl has been desperately ill," confided Margot to her as they lay beside each other in their deck chairs, "and I'm ashamed to say that I am completely worn out by nursing her, so my husband insisted on this trip — oh yes, she is quite recovered by now, thank you, but I'm afraid I'm not too good about heat. They said April would be all right — it's my cabin, you see, isn't yours quite terrible too?"

It proved much less so, bigger and with a fan that worked. "It's just too bad, your little girl having been so sick. I guess I'm first cousin to a salamander, heat never seems to trouble me. Now, Margot — I may call you Margot, mayn't I? and I'm Dimity — why shouldn't we change cabins? I've not properly unpacked — now don't say 'no'."

"Oh, but I must," said Margot, "I couldn't possibly let you." But she found it was possible after all.

It had been a relief to get away from Cairo, which

Margot thought hideous, noisy and full of beggars, but it seemed there was no more to be seen before Luxor, which would take five days to reach, during which time there was nothing to do but sit about on the deck watching the long endless river banks slip slowly by and eat the rather unappetizing food which apparently, nostalgically trying to ape the menus of a Victorian schoolroom, consisted of too much meat, too few vegetables, and milk puddings. "Don't touch the salads," warned Miss Benson, the experienced BBC producer who sat at their table.

The English-speaking party consisted of Dimity and her married sister and husband — the sister, Holly, was slightly larger and both wore enormous pale-rimmed spectacles which made them look like a pair of starved owls. There were, besides, an elderly retired Civil Servant closely resembling Alec Guinness, with a small waspish French wife, two knowledgeable school teachers, Crispin and his wife Prue. The rest of the tourists were Germans and Dutch who kept to themselves.

The weather was excessively hot, unusually so they were assured. The slow motion of the boat, the unvarying light and landscape, produced in Margot a sense of unreality as if she were viewing, or even herself part of, a monotonous film, and Crispin, who should have brought everything to life, was proving the second and more insidious disappointment. He had behaved as she had expected, the affair between them had developed as she had intended, but their love-making seemed disconcertingly irrelevant, as if he too were a degree removed from reality.

Then there was Prue — Margot had been disconcerted at first that Crispin, who had assured her that he could find someone to take Andrew's place to keep Prue amused, had apparently not bothered to do this, but she soon concluded that it had not really been necessary. Prue not only accepted the situation but seemed relieved by it.

126

"I bore him, you know, and it is so important for him not to be bored." Dimity took Prue under her wing and soon knew more about both her and Crispin than Margot had ever known or cared to know.

"She sure comes from one of your real old families, the kind that don't appreciate Art unless it's ancient and hung in their galleries, and they didn't care for her to take up with it. But she had money of her own and she quit, and she and he were studying together in London — but you sure know all this, Margot. Well, don't you agree it's a shame she's given it all up? She was doing fine, just loved painting flower pieces, I bet they were real pretty; he said so too, he said they were cute. That ought to obligate her to continue, shouldn't it? Because he must know. She could do some pretty views right now, I tell her."

What pretty views? thought Margot drearily. *Shaggy banana trees with bananas growing the wrong way up, repetitive palm trees and flat green strips of land backed by the ever-lasting sand.*

Prue didn't talk, she generally had a book for company. "It's too hot even to read, I think," said Margot. "What have you got there?"

"Nothing that matters," said Prue hastily.

"Prue enjoys Edwardian fiction," remarked Crispin. He made it sound like an addiction to dominoes. She was often inclined to be vague and unpunctual. "I can't think why you can't wear a watch like other people," said Crispin.

There was something in the way Prue used to look at him and the tone of his voice when he spoke to her that seemed familiar to Margot, but the train of thought was somehow distasteful and she did not pursue it. Her relationship with Crispin became less and less satisfactory. Her meetings with him in London had been accompanied by good food and drink, and generally diversified

127

with some entertainment to follow, but now she found long stretches of talk with him more and more wearying. There was a central point in their conversation from which everything radiated and to which everything returned, and this was Crispin Keylock and not Margot Royce. She felt herself growing less charming and less charmed, and at length Crispin appeared to feel this too, for he turned more and more to others of their party and especially to Boone Cleveland, Dimity's brother-in-law. Boone was impressed to learn that Crispin Keylock was an avant-garde sculptor who had held successful exhibitions in London and Paris and whose portrait busts were beginning to be sought after.

"Tell me, Mr Keylock," he said one evening, "how can an ordinary guy like me get to appreciate what fellows like you are getting at? I just would like to support you but I want to know what I'm paying my money for."

Quick on the scent, Crispin braced himself to reply in his most professional vein.

"For myself," he said, "I feel I perform, as it were, a holding operation between the concept and the media. Don't you agree it is the job, to put it no higher, of 'fellows like myself', as you say, to establish the insightful on both points? Conceptually, you see, the public — if I may include you under that umbrella? but you have placed yourself there — ."

"I sure did," agreed Boone Cleveland.

"Well, as you say, quite naturally and honestly, you do need us to mediate; after all, that's what the words imply when all's said and done."

Boone nodded.

"You have abstract emotion on the one hand," said Crispin warming up, "totally unacceptable, wouldn't you say? And yet utterly indispensable, and the ritual forms of aesthetic experience, including — one must absolutely these days strike out for the all-inclusive — the

Royal Academy for instance."

Boone clutched at the Royal Academy.

"A fine show," he said, "Holly and I visited it last time we were over."

"Well yes, the all-inclusive, as I was saying," continued Crispin, "and that does of course include both the Royal Academy and the public urinal via that vital participant, the *individual*. That's where portraiture comes in, so often a chat show these days as you must have noticed. But in my work, Mr Cleveland, I do see myself actually as an interviewer in what I consider as the great straight tradition on the box."

Boone Cleveland was visibly impressed, though not much elucidated.

"I'd sure like to see some of your work, Mr Keylock," he said.

"I think my wife has some photos with her somewhere," said Crispin, "if you really would care to look at them."

The photographs were produced. Clipped to one of them was a laudatory review of an exhibition.

"Oh yes," said Crispin casually, "I'd forgotten that was there, unaccountably the critics this time did seem to see what I was after."

"Read it out, Boone," said Dimity, peering at the prints. "It's gotta help!"

Boone Cleveland read: " 'Crispin Keylock conveys the ominously indicative with a rare blend of nonchalance and holistic expertise suggesting that here at least we have an acceptable equivalent of Nouveau Beaujolais which has a lotta bottle and may well stand the test of time, specially in 'Portrait of a Taxpayer' and 'Mood No. twenty-one'. Eclecticism is by no means a pejorative phrase in the right hands. His skilful use of polystyrene and titanium to convey overtones of despair are especially successful.' "

129

"Well," exclaimed Dimity after a little pause, "isn't that fine!"

"Which is the Taxpayer, have you got one of him?" asked Holly.

"Yes," said Crispin, "you've got him there."

"Doesn't look too good to go to bed with," said Holly, "all that wire."

"Now, Holly!" reproved her husband. "We must have you over in the States, Mr Keylock," he continued, "I think I can promise you you'll be appreciated there, and I'd be proud to help you all I can."

"You know, I've a good mind to take him up on that," said Crispin to Margot afterwards, "it might not be at all a bad thing."

Margot agreed, but Andrew's dismissal of Crispin as "not a serious artist" recurred to her as his remarks often had a habit of doing, however irritating at the time. What was a serious artist anyway? Well, Boone Cleveland was willing to back Crispin, obviously differing from Andrew, and he was certainly beginning to make a name for himself, which was good for her art gallery, she supposed.

At last the boat reached Luxor and they disembarked and went by donkey carriages to the Temple of Karnak. Here Margot's sense of unreality intensified — the vast columns and statues diminished her almost to vanishing point. Awe invaded her like a dark cloud, blotting out all familiarities. She recovered a little at Tutankhamun's tomb, which was smaller and less impressive than she had expected, and where the garish paintings partially dispelled the awe. But the expeditions during the days that followed were filled with inexorable ruins. The Germans and Americans, bristling with notebooks and cameras, asked endless questions of the incomprehensible Egyptian guides, and the dark steps, the subterranean tombs, affected Margot like a miasma. Before they reached Aswan she became ill. It was easy

130

enough, Miss Benson had said, to pick up a bug, as everything unmentionable went into the river. She had bouts of sickness and diarrhoea. Cardboard figures of Crispin, Prue and Dimity hovered about her. Crispin brought a huge bunch of scarlet objects pretending to be flowers from which she tried to hide. She slept most of the time with a recurring nightmare that she saw herself at Karnak again, a minute figure running down an unending passage between the monotonous columns. Far away in front of her was a patch of mirage brightness, in the centre of which she seemed to glimpse the quivering image of a house — of the Lotus House — but she knew she would never reach it, and the pitch of horror came when she was forced to watch the tiny figure disintegrate into nothingness.

After two days the attack wore off and she struggled out very early in the morning to catch a breath of coolness and lay hidden in a corner on the deck. She had fallen half asleep again when the sound of her own name woke her immediately. She recognised the voices of the Civil Servant and his wife.

"I wonder how that pretty Mrs Royce is doing. They say she has been quite unwell. She should have a husband here to look after her."

"In more ways than one," said his wife.

"You mean that posturing sculptor fellow — yes, that's a pity, and there's the little wife too."

"You distress yourself unnecessarily, chérie — the wife was swallowed up long ago, she no longer exists, and as for the beautiful lady and the artist, that will not last long, they are too much of the same portmanteau, two beans in a row, how do you say it?"

"I say 'peas in a pod', my dear; but how do you make *that* out?"

"Both are *tout à fait égoistes*."

The voices faded away as they moved off, leaving

131

Margot surprised by the intensity of the anger that possessed her. She was not in the least like Crispin — the woman was a fool, not worth thinking about. But she continued to think about her furiously. It became absolutely necessary to refute her, and now she found herself unaccountably arguing the case with Andrew.

"All right, I give it to you about Crispin, but you must see that Frenchwoman's quite, quite wrong. I'm *always* aware of other people, you say too much so, *he's* only aware of himself, and look how he treats Prue." Suddenly the half-recognized familiarity in Crispin's tone as he spoke to his wife, and of her answering look, thrust itself once more into her consciousness — this time with greater clarity and she did not like the revelation at all. "That's utterly different," she said. But now the sun had crept round to her corner and she went back to her cabin.

They were nearing Aswan and it seemed hotter than ever, but at Aswan the cruise would be over. "My next holiday abroad will be among snow mountains," decided Margot. "Switzerland, I think, the cleanest and tidiest place I know."

At Aswan everybody else went to see more ruins in a felucca, but Margot drove through sandy poverty-stricken streets to a grotesquely grand hotel, where they were to spend the night and where, with a totally unexpected eagerness, she hoped to find some mail.

"I daresay you won't want letters and I daresay I shan't write," Andrew had said, "but you'd better leave an address in case." There was a letter but she saw with disappointment that it was addressed in Harriet's unformed script.

"Dear Margot," she read, "I can cook, Andrew says I do sossages and bacon very well. We put all the things back in the wrong places. Andrew says when the cat's away the mice do play. We went to a consert. Love and kisses, Harriet. P.T.O." Margot turned the page quickly, but there was only the briefest of postscripts. "Greetings, my serpent of old Nile, Harriet's fine. Andrew."

"Why does he call me a serpent?" said Margot, angry to find her eyes filling with tears of disappointment and self-pity, "The weakness still from that horrid attack, I suppose." She read Harriet's letter again, really, it was hardly worth sending. "He might at least have seen that she spelt it properly." But there was a new note in it quite unlike any letter she had had from Harriet before. *I hope the child's not being a bore*, she thought, *it sounds rather as if she is*.

Andrew, however, was not at all bored. Letty Sanderson thought the trouble he was taking over Harriet showed true kindness. Margot would have supposed him to be carrying out some kind of psychological experiment in his usual detached manner. It was neither of these. He was actually and unexpectedly simply enjoying himself, he was discovering the pleasure of communication. It was necessary to explain and to comment to Harriet on many things, which to him had become merely commonplaces, and this gave them fresh value. After Harriet had gone to bed, he sometimes found himself ruminating, not about her but about himself. He knew himself, both in temperament and experience, to be lacking in the practice of communication, he had not hitherto felt the need, in fact he considered it hazardous. The lunchtime concert he had taken Harriet to was in an eighteenth-century church. "It isn't a bit like a church," she had said. She was right, thought Andrew, it was too calm, too lucid, prayer here would be irrelevant, in a building that accomplished perfection by exclusion. Was it an analogy of his own aims and ideas? Hitherto he had gone his own way, with a fair amount of good humour admittedly — but that was just the luck of his genes. You couldn't go your way so completely with a child however, and though it was only for so short a time, the commitment necessary was a new

133

experience. He was conditioned by training to pay attention to fresh phenomena and examined his reactions with interest. They were mixed — he saw with apprehension cracks appearing in his carefully constructed attitudes, but the cracks undeniably let in new light. After which musings he would play a little Bach and take himself off to bed. One evening he gave his parents a ring, realizing he had not made contact with them for months. They seemed pleased, if surprised, and he arranged for a meeting in the near future.

"You'd like this house," he said.

When Margot arrived back Harriet was out having tea with Miss Johnson.

"Hullo, darling," said Andrew, "I didn't expect you so early, the plane must have been punctual for once."

"You didn't think of meeting me, I suppose," said Margot.

"I never meet people unless they've been away for at least a year," said Andrew.

"It seems like a hundred years," said Margot, "but I don't suppose you'd have missed me however long I'd been. I expect if some Arab sheik had abducted me, you'd have merely said 'how interesting'."

"No," said Andrew, "I wouldn't, but it would have been all the same."

"Oh, you're hopeless," said Margot, with a sort of sob.

"Yes," said Andrew — but looking up at her quickly and with surprise, "I'm hopeless and so are you, and that's where the fun begins."

"Does it?" said Margot, "I don't call it fun."

"Try," said Andrew, "you and Harriet take life too seriously, and I'm beginning to think I've never taken it on at all."

"What *are* you talking about?" said Margot.

Andrew kissed her. "Let's get married," he said, "I'm sure this house is the sort that would appreciate a respectable married couple."

Margot turned away from him but Andrew crossed the room and put on a dance record, caught her to him and whirled her about the room.

With a sudden overwhelming sense of having reached home at last, Margot capitulated. They spun round ever more madly, yet, in her heart, there was an extraordinary stillness and peace.

It won't last, of course, thought her parents' daughter. *But it will come again*, thought Andrew's love, *and anyway, I've known it and I'll remember it for ever*, thought Margot.

As they were still dancing, Harriet came in. She stood astonished while the music slowed to a halt.

"Put on the other side, Harriet," shouted Andrew, "we don't want to stop yet and we'll have to without your help."

Harriet did as she was told and then Margot, by way of greeting, put out a hand and caught her up with the two of them in the dance.

135

CHAPTER ELEVEN

THAT SPRING PASSED in a grey mist as far as Aubrey Stacey's state of mind was concerned. Since Harriet's visit to his attic and the night that had followed, he had no longer hated nor feared his so-called pupils, he simply accepted the fact that he did not have either the personality or the skills needed to deal with them. Hassan had not appeared for his second term; his father had found a better job in another district. On learning this Aubrey felt a dull relief. He had reached a sort of compromise with his classes; perhaps they sensed that he was no longer antagonistic or even desirous of putting up a fight. At any rate, they ceased to torment him but merely stonewalled any attempt on his part to make them work. He went through the motions of teaching like an automaton and the front row "snobs" had to make the best of it.

During the Easter break he resolved to get down to his magnum opus in earnest and filled a notebook with period data. He was classifying and neatly copying out these for easy reference one afternoon, a job he enjoyed, when he was disturbed by a knock on his door and, opening it, was surprised to see his brother on the threshold.

"Michael!" he exclaimed, "What brings you here?"

"Bad news, I'm afraid, Mole." It was the old nickname, dating from childhood days when, under the spell of *The Wind in the Willows*, they had been Ratty and Mole to each other. The names had outlived the nursery and even school and were still sometimes used, especially by Michael.

"Come in," said Aubrey, and he led the way to his sitting-room, pushed a chair forward and sat down himself by the open window, as if he needed air.

"It's Father and Mother," said Michael, "the police phoned me this morning. . . an accident with a lorry on the motorway."

"Serious?" asked Aubrey, but he knew the answer.

"Very, I'm afraid — it was instantaneous."

"Both?"

Michael nodded and the brothers remained silent for what seemed to Aubrey a long time as he looked from the window, noting meticulously the clouds drifting high in the pale sky, and the brilliant green of the new chestnut leaves.

Then Michael said: "There were no witnesses and the driver of the lorry escaped, but the evidence, such as it is, seems to confirm that it was not his fault, or at least not wholly so. Father shouldn't really have been still driving; his reactions had slowed up but he so hated any suggestion that he should give it up. It's hard to take it in, isn't it? They were both so active still. Mother was with us very recently and we were out and about a lot."

Aubrey said, "I haven't seen them for a good while."

"No, well, time goes by so quickly," said Michael, "and one is always so busy. Can I have a drink?"

"Yes, of course," said Aubrey, but he made no move to get it, and it was Michael who poured them both one and took Aubrey his.

"Nice place you've got here," he said, "a good view."

"Yes," said Aubrey. The detached remark had cleared the overcharged atmosphere a little and he got up. "My bedroom's really the better room. Come and see it."

"Facing south," said Michael approvingly, "I like a

south bedroom, but whyever the bars? I suppose it must have been a nursery once. Why didn't you have them taken down? They spoil the outlook." And then, not waiting for an answer, he went on: "Funny how old this makes you feel all of a sudden, isn't it? I suppose one's parents are always a sort of bulwark against old age and death and now the barrier's down. Well, there's a lot to see about, of course, and Julia and I hope you'll come back with us. It's holidays still, isn't it? If you've nothing special, on perhaps you could come straight away?"

Aubrey assented at once. He put away his papers and went to pack a bag. On his chest-of-drawers stood the photographs of his father and mother in a double frame. Looking at them, Aubrey felt the first real pang of emotion. They had already taken on that remote alien quality that always seemed to belong to the portraits of the dead, and it struck him that he would now never be able to prove his true worth to them. It was this sense of negation that substituted itself for any real grief. He had not encountered death on intimate terms before, and it was its monstrous impossibility that stunned him. This impression did not weaken in the days that followed. He behaved and spoke as he was expected to behave and speak, at the funeral, and at the gathering of friends and relatives afterwards but beneath this façade there was nothing but disbelief. How could anyone who was alive believe in death? Where *were* his parents? Their absence in their own home was extraordinary. Why did he not hear their voices or their footsteps? Everything expected them — all the household objects, their favourite chairs, their clothes, their shoes — his father's sticks in the hall, his mother's gardening gloves. There was dust on the mantelpiece where his mother had never allowed dust, that was an outrage. When no one was looking he took out his handkerchief and removed it. But he knew that the emotion he was feeling was different from his

138

brother's — it was largely impersonal. The nearest he got to anything closer was the gratitude he felt towards his father when his will made it clear that no difference was to be made between himself and his brother, the elder by half an hour. But gratitude is not grief.

The house was to be put up for sale, and Michael and he met together there again later to settle what they wanted to keep of its contents. Aubrey only wished for some of his father's books and a fine chiming clock which he had always admired.

"Are you sure you won't reserve anything else?" asked Michael.

"Quite sure. I've not room in my flat, for one thing."

"But you may marry and want to set up a home," said Michael, but Aubrey shook his head.

"I shall never marry," he said decisively.

"Well, anyway, Julia and I have got plenty of storage space and it's a shame to let so much go to strangers; I shall take some extra pieces and you can draw on us if the time comes that you need them."

The brothers finished their last look round and went out together. The door clicked to behind them and Michael said, "Well, Mole, I suppose we may never come here again — how strange that is."

"Very strange," said Aubrey, "wonderfully strange," he repeated to himself. Gradually the enormity of death had receded and a feeling of profound ease had taken its place — an inapt ease and a lightness of spirit.

"I wish you'd come and pay us a proper visit soon," said Michael, "we don't manage to see enough of each other somehow."

"Thank you, Ratty," said Aubrey, "I will."

There were only a few days of the holidays left now and he had decided to give in his notice as soon as the term had begun, for there would be enough from his father's estate to enable him to devote himself to his writing, at least for some time to come. On the evening after he had got back to the Lotus House, he settled down to his manuscript once more.

"I'll go over the whole thing again first, to get into the right mood for tackling the next part. I've got enough notes I know, but in a big work one has to be careful to maintain consistency of plot and characters". So much had happened since he had begun the novel that he could hardly remember details of the early chapters, only the glow with which he had conceived the whole enterprise. But, as he read his neatly typed pages, the realization grew relentlessly upon him that their glory had departed. It had apparently only existed in his imagination. The book was a study in monochrome, lacking even the neon-lighting of melodrama; the characters, stuffed into their historical roles as if into fancy dress, had never come to life. There were long passages of guidebook description interspersed with sudden bursts of inconsistent action. It was lamentable! Well, no, now he was going to the other extreme — some of it wasn't so bad, but still it would not do, he saw very clearly that it would not do.

"I'm a failure as a creative writer as well as a teacher," he declared, but the declaration was almost triumphant. "It doesn't matter though, it simply doesn't matter any more." This discovery was extraordinarily exhilarating. On the top of his desk were arranged all his research notebooks — *It's a pity to waste all that I must say*, he thought, *perhaps I'll produce that monograph on old Cotton one of these days, yes, I think I might make quite a good job of that, but what on earth else shall I do?* His eyes wandered round the room as if for a clue, they dwelt lovingly as usual on his books. *I must put up some more shelves for Father's*, he thought. There were two packing-cases of these waiting on the landing.

Then inspiration came — "Of course, that's what drew me to Cotton, the great librarian, in the first place.

I'll take a librarian's course and live happy and humdrum ever after. In my spare time I'll write my monographs and edit texts. 'Nuns fret not at their convent's narrow room, and hermits are contented with their cells,' " he quoted, "and why not, I should like to know." He looked again at the magnum opus lying in confusion all over his desk and felt the need for some symbolic act. "I'd like to burn it and see the silly dream vanishing up the chimney in smoke, but that's the worst of an electric fire. I think I'll borrow a spade, yes, 'bury it certain fathoms in the earth' like Prospero's book, only I'm not a Prospero and never have been." For the present however, he shovelled all the chapters back into the drawer. The end of *The Tempest* was drifting through his mind as he did so. He had a less difficult task than Prospero, after all — it is easier to forgive the dead.

It was getting late, his father's clock chimed midnight and a new day was beginning as Aubrey went to his bed. *I'll get those bars taken down*, was his last thought before he went to sleep, *Michael was right about them, they do obscure the view*.

The bars were duly removed and one warm May afternoon Aubrey was able, by leaning out, to see the first wisteria blooms here and there between their pale patterned leaves. Further down beneath them he caught sight of Miss Cook bent over her border, assiduously weeding and planting.

It was not an uncommon sight, for Janet Cook's grandfather's genes had been ever more busily asserting themselves since she had taken over the strip of garden allotted to her by Mrs Sanderson. The box she had once labelled "Sitting-room new carpet fund" was not getting any heavier, for all her spare cash seemed now to go in providing herself with garden tools, sprays and fertilizers, not to speak of seeds, bulbs and plants. She was a regular listener to "Gardeners' Question Time" and viewer of

141

"Gardeners' World" and this did not, with her, result in envy or despondency but in inspiration and achievement. She was rewarded. All her plants behaved well and did what was required of them, making sturdy but not ill-mannered growth both outside and in the house for, emulating Dian, she soon had a row of healthy pot plants on the broad window-sills behind the pink curtains. Letty Sanderson, on the other hand, admitted sadly to herself that though she loved flowers, her plants didn't seem to like her much! "It's because I'm sentimental over them," she sighed; "sentimental", a dirty word nowadays, could, she feared, be applied to her in general. It was awful to be sentimental and know it: if one didn't know it, it could make one happy. Anyway she was afraid she really was very sentimental over flowers. She adored their beauty but often forgot to water them, and then to make up for it she watered them too much, and of course that made them bad-tempered. So bad-tempered that they died just to spite her, she thought, as she threw out what had once been a splendid cyclamen given to her by Margot in gratitude for her help with Harriet after the accident. Margot had made a similar presentation to Miss Cook — she had got them cheap from the firm that supplied decorative plants to her art gallery. Janet's cyclamen, of course, had flourished and the lovely but-terfly blossoms would probably renew themselves for years to come, thought Letty, and having seen how successfully the basement border had been cultivated, she had asked Janet to extend and broaden this, and there was now quite a sizeable little sunny flower-garden beneath and beyond the balcony. So, in this second summer, as Aubrey Stacey looked out from his window, he could smell, in addition to the wisteria, the warm late wallflowers and the early fragrant pinks. He could also see a neat edging of deep blue forget-me-nots and a clump of single white peonies just coming into flower. Later,

142

there would be sweetpeas and roses and just now Janet was busy with her summer planting, snapdragons and petunias and stocks and, in the sunniest spot, a row of zinnias. She had raised all these from seed in what had once been the old scullery and here, too, she kept during the winter the cuttings she had taken from her geraniums and pelargoniums. She loved these. "Anyone's welcome to all that greenery," she had said derisively once to Dian, who was describing admiringly the fashionable trailing spider plant that Margot had lately established on the landing of the first floor flat — "a bit of colour for me!"

"Well, that there geranium with a '*p*' does you credit, I must say," admitted Dian. It was a splendid purple and white pelargonium, the queen of all her pot plants, and had actually been the first she had ever brought. Miss Budgeon of the little corner shop had embarked on a small stand of plants and flowers, squeezed between the fruit and vegetables. Influenced by Miss Sanderson, all the tenants of the Lotus House patronized the corner shop, and one day Janet Cook, after having purchased a nice little cauliflower, found herself transfixed by a vision of glory. It was the finest pelargonium she had ever encountered. She looked at the price and turned away. She was not yet a fully committed addict and the carpet box beckoned. But those extravagantly rich purple and white flowers danced before her eyes all day and were a trouble to her dreams by night. She resisted all the rest of the week, but on Saturday morning she gave in and, in a panic lest the plant should have been sold, she rifled the carpet-fund box and almost ran to the shop, returning guilty but triumphant.

"Wasting all that money on a flower," said her mother.

Of course the pelargonium flourished in superb health; and in the late summer she had taken two cuttings from it and cossetted them through the winter months and now

143

they were putting forth strong shoots.

Afterwards Janet always felt annoyed that it was Dian and not herself who had first discovered something odd about one of the cuttings. She was showing them off and pointing out that each had two fat buds when Dian said, "I thought they were purple and white."

"So they are," said Janet.

"Well, this one's different," said Dian, "looks funny to me, a kind of grey, see?"

Janet saw — and it *was* distinctly different from the other cutting, the bud tips of which already showed the correct hue, yet it was just as healthy. Janet gave it a little extra feed and pushed it into the sunniest corner.

On Dian's next Tuesday she found Janet waiting to waylay her.

"She was really over the moon, she was," Dian told Luke that evening, "her eyes popping out — well they do pop a bit most times, but this time I thought they was just like my Monday lady's peke, so I went along with her as quick as I could, though I ought really to have been doing the drawing-room floor. 'It's my pel . . . ' whatever it's called, she said, 'it's going to be a blue one and I don't believe there's never been a blue one before.' Well, it wasn't what I'd call proper blue, more airforce, if you know what I mean, but you could stretch a point. 'Oo,' I says, 'it might be goin' to make your fortune, what did your stars say this week, did you look at them?' But she never does, careless I call it. What d'you think, Luke?"

"I dunno, honey, flowers is your concern, but you tell her to take advice, there'll be those who'll know."

By the time Dian saw Janet again she had already taken the pelargonium to Miss Budgeon to show her the blue flower. Miss Budgeon belonged to the local horticultural society and had tried to get Janet to join. "I don't join things," was all the response she had had hitherto. Lately, however, Janet had secretly been weakening. There were lectures and shows and gardening stock to be had at a discount and it didn't seem fair to her flowers somehow to keep out of it. Now she felt the need both for information and encouragement. Miss Budgeon, for instance, was full of sympathetic interest in Janet's blue blossoms.

"You really should join our society, Miss Cook," she said, "there's our summer show coming off next month and there's a special class for last year's cuttings."

It'll mean mixing with a lot of strangers, thought Janet dubiously, *still it may be my duty in a manner of speaking*. Miss Budgeon produced the necessary forms for her to fill up and she decided that, besides entering her pelargonium, she would also compete for the best nosegay of annuals and for the sweetpea section as well. Roses were chancy, if you only had a few bushes, you couldn't count on any blooms being just at the right stage, whereas her sweetpeas promised very well.

"In for a penny, in for a pound," said Janet to herself, and it really turned out to be several points on her right side, for her posy of cornflowers and clarkia and larkspur and pansies was awarded a third prize, her sweetpeas a second, and a first with special distinction for her pelargonium, now proudly displaying no less than three blue blooms.

The judge, a BBC personality called Tom Austen, presented the prizes and when it came to Janet's turn he detained her.

"As a member of the Geranium and Pelargonium Society, Miss Cook, I am very intrigued by your blue flowering plant. You have grown it from a cutting, I see. Have you been experimenting with different varieties long?"

"Oh, no," said Janet, "I haven't experimented at all, it just came like that. As a matter of fact, I am not an experienced gardener, I had never grown anything till I retired two years ago."

"Really!" said Tom Austen. "And you've run away with three prizes, quite a record I should think. I congratulate you and if you will allow me, I would very much like to keep in touch on behalf of the society with regard to your interesting sport."

Janet gave a grudging consent. "Letting a strange man have your name and address like that," exclaimed her mother.

"You see," Miss Budgeon had explained afterwards, "they'll want to find out whether more blue pelargoniums can be grown from yours, and if they can, Miss Cook, you might become quite famous."

When Janet got home after the show she put all her prize money into the carpet-fund box which had been so neglected and even robbed. It was a kind of placation; she was determined not to spend any more on the garden, just at the present. It was as well not to tempt fortune, there were always snags about. All the same, she felt very proud, it had been an amazing day, perhaps the most exciting she could remember, and even more extraordinary things were to follow.

About two weeks later, her phone rang and a voice, a polite, pleasant, voice enquired if it could speak to Miss Janet Cook.

"Who is it?" asked Janet cautiously.

"My name is Cassie Kay," said the voice, "I'm from the BBC and I would very much like to speak to Miss Janet Cook."

"Speaking," said Janet.

"Oh, good morning, Miss Cook," said Cassie Kay, "we are doing a short series on BBC1 telivision called "Senior Starters", aimed as its name implies primarily at the active retired category, but of course we hope of interest to a wider circle. It comes on on Tuesdays at 7.10 p.m. Perhaps you have seen it? No — well, Tom Austen tells us you have taken up gardening since your retirement

146

and have produced a new species of geranium. It seems to us that you might make a valuable contribution to our series, if you would allow us to make a short film of you in your garden and with your wonderful plant."

There was a pause.

"Well, I don't know, I'm sure," said Janet at last, "I never thought of such a thing."

This was an understatement. "A bolt from the blue," she said afterwards, "that's what it was, a regular bolt from the blue."

There was another pause, but only a short one this time. "You would like to think it over, of course," said the beguiling voice of Cassie Kay, "perhaps I could ring you tomorrow. I do so hope you'll say 'yes', Miss Cook. I'll ring tomorrow evening if that is convenient. Goodbye for the present then."

Janet was flustered and apprehensive, but beneath this there burned a small flame of glory. She decided to consult Mrs Sanderson. It was right to do so anyway, she couldn't very well let photographers and who-knows-what descend on the Lotus House unbeknown to its owner.

"But how lovely!" exclaimed Letty. "I do congratulate you. Dian had told me about your geranium and I have been meaning to ask you if I could see it. Now tell me all about it, please, from the beginning."

"It's what they call a sport," said Janet, "the parent plant was purple and white, I got it from Miss Budgeon's shop."

"Oh," said Letty, "that explains it, that shop has always dealt in magic.'"

Janet thought, *How silly Mrs Sanderson is sometimes, but there, she's getting on after all.*

However, the conversation with Letty somehow settled it, and so it came about that one morning what seemed like a perfect army of strangers descended upon Miss Cook at the Lotus House basement flat and took over. It

147

was this sensation of being taken over that was the strongest impression left with Janet when the day was done. She was posed standing in the middle of her garden, walking up the path, picking flowers and lastly in her sitting room holding her pelargonium.

"A fine house this," the photographer had commented, "it's a bonus as a background. May we just trouble you once more, from a little distance this time, so as to concentrate on a good picture of the whole building . . . That's splendid, thank you so much, Miss Cook, I think this will make a really rewarding film."

"I just wish it had been me," said Dian. "Didn't it make you feel like the Queen?"

"I don't know what the Queen feels like," said Janet tartly. "It made *me* feel silly."

"What did they say?" enquired Dian. "Some of them interviewers are lovely, but some can be horrible, only Luke says they don't mean no harm really."

"This one wasn't horrible," admitted Janet, "just stupid."

"How d'yer mean stupid?" asked Dian, shocked.

"Asking questions nobody could answer like, "How does it feel, Miss Cook, to have made the desert blossom like the rose?' " said Janet in a mincing voice.

"I call that pretty," said Dian, "like something out of a musical."

"It's out of the Bible," said Janet.

"What did you say?" persisted Dian.

"I said 'It's good loam soil, not at all sandy.' And then they asked me what I was going to call my new wonderful blue variety, and I said it might never do it again and I wasn't one to count my chickens before they were hatched."

"Well," said Dian reproachfully, "you weren't very kind to the poor chap, was you? He was only trying to get you to talk nice."

148

"It can't be helped now," said Janet. "I dare say I was a bit short. It's not what I'm used to, you see."

Janet was informed that the film would be shown in three weeks' time. She debated whether to let Henry and Doris know. She hadn't told them anything at all as yet, not even about the flower show and the pelargonium. She didn't want Doris interfering and she couldn't tell how Henry would take it. Finally she decided it would be mean not to say anything. Besides they'd be sure to get to know, though she didn't think they would look at the programme unless they were told. But people always did get to know things when you didn't want them to. So she sent them a picture postcard of Westminster Abbey just before the great day and wrote on it: "Don't miss 'Senior Starters' BBC1 Tuesday 7.10, love Janet." *I'm sure they'll be too curious not to look and when they do they'll get the shock of their lives*, she thought with satisfaction as she posted it. She could just see their faces.

Everyone else knew. "I can't wait!" said Dian. "Mind you come home in time, Luke. You ought to've heard her telling off that interviewer, ever so cheeky, she was."

"I expect they'll cut it, they mostly cuts half of what they make you say," said Luke.

"Seems funny when you comes to think of it," said Dian, "all those people all over, going to hear her and to see her and when I first knows her, there she was darting away behind her door, scared to show herself just to me. Not much of the goldfish left now."

CHAPTER TWELVE

IT IS A fact, and not a very admirable one, that a person or a building or a landscape that is familiar to oneself, if it is to be seen in a photograph or on the television screen, takes on a compelling interest. Although probably not one of the inhabitants of the Lotus House would have bothered to look at a travel film that might have enlarged their visual experience and added to their knowledge, all were glued to the box on that summer evening to see Miss Cook, her garden and her plant against the background of their own home, which they could have seen, and indeed did see, any and every day much better in reality.

Letty had thought it might have been pleasant if they could have watched the film together, but Janet Cook had said, "It's kind of you, Mrs Sanderson, but I don't fancy seeing myself in public somehow. I mean it's not natural, is it, if you see what I mean."

Letty thought she did see and did not press it. Then there was Aubrey Stacey, he too thanked her politely but said that he was afraid he really couldn't bear colour television — it was an idiosyncrasy for which he apologized, but there it was, and he really would prefer to see the film on his own set as he knew he was in a small minority and couldn't expect people to turn off their colour for him. After that Letty gave up. She knew the Royces had a bigger and better television than hers.

Janet Cook sat upright on the edge of her grandfather's chair gripping its arms. She could not have described her state of mind — "queer", that's all she could have said, "definitely queer." Wasn't there a story about someone meeting himself one day and getting quite a shock? She could believe it. Why had she let herself in for all this? *You've only yourself to blame, Janet*, but this never made things easier — one could often enjoy blaming others.

Well, now it was time and, pressing her thin little lips even more tightly together, she got up and switched on, and there she was already, coming straight down the garden path right at her, only it wasn't herself after all, it was her mother. She would have known her anywhere, but of course it couldn't be, it must be her. She supposed that through the years her own face had become too familiar to be seen any more, and because her hair at least was still black, she hadn't realized that now she looked quite old, a bit shrunk and bent and decidedly skinny. Why, she was more like her mother than Henry after all, because of course they were both women. But now that other Janet was stopping and looking down at her flowers — this was when they had asked her to pick some. She was stooping down to choose which to take, but you could still see her face, and, staring at it, the one Janet saw the face of the other change, it wasn't her mother's face any longer. Who did it remind her of? She couldn't think at first, then a long buried memory flashed upon her, her father looking down on her, a very little girl and saying: "Coming for a walk with me, little 'un?" "Who'd have thought it?" said Janet aloud to the empty room: "Poor old Dad."

But now the talking began. *Well, I've never heard that voice before in all my life*, thought Janet indignantly, *they must have done something to it*. She simply couldn't pay attention to what was being said — the squeaky, jerky

151

tone of her own speech, like a ventriloquist's doll, horrified her. Then the scene changed again and there she was holding up her pelargonium in the sitting-room. Well, that at least was all right, splendid it looked, and the last pictures were really pretty. She suddenly decided she would ask Mrs Sanderson to let her have still a bit more ground this autumn — that piece by the garages, she'd plant it out with flowering shrubs to hide them, you could get lovely ones nowadays. And now came the last shot of all, the one taken at a little distance with the whole house in and all her flowers in front. A flood of pride and satisfaction invaded her. Perhaps hundreds and hundreds of people were seeing the garden she had made and were enjoying it. She felt her heart expand to take them all in.

Had it not been for Mrs Sanderson, Aubrey would not have even known about the programme, and but for Dian would probably have forgotten to look at it. Dian had written a note with the red felt pen he used for correcting his school exercise books and had left it for him, propped up by his clock. It said: "Mr Stacey, don't you forget, 7.10 this evening, Miss Cook on TV as ever is. Dian."

Dian had adopted a protective attitude towards him lately. "Poor chap," she had said to Letty, "losing his parents like that. I remember when Mum went, you feels all cold. I went on feeling cold, really, right on till I met my Luke, but it's sobered him up no end, nothing like the bottles to clear out nowadays. Funny isn't it? Took my brother Fred right the other way — well, it takes all sorts."

Aubrey seldom used his television set and had to clear away a pile of books that had accumulated in front of it. He considered watching a waste of time and really thought it so now, for he wasn't much interested either in flowers or Miss Cook, but he felt it would be discourteous to ignore both Mrs Sanderson and Dian's recommendation, and also even he was not immune from the strange fascination of seeing the familiar reproduced by the media. Afterwards he was glad he had done so, for he had noticed something about the house that he had not known was there before. Over his bedroom window was carved a second lotus flower similar to the one above the front entrance. He supposed the bars had obscured the view of it before. He began to wonder why the carvings were there. He had once asked Mrs Sanderson about it, but she could tell him little. She had some vague romantic story of a connection of the house with the East, but she did not seem to want to follow this up or to transform it into anything more substantial. He began to muse over the mythology connected with the Lotus. It seemed, as far as he could make out, ambiguous. There was the classical association through Homer of the sinister compelling magic that had inspired Tennyson's *Lotus Eaters* — the false dreams of a hollow land — but the Eastern Lotus of Vishnu and Buddha was life-giving, a vision of creative energy and truth, whose emblem was the white lily rising from the dark waters. Was this the house of fantasy or of vision, or perhaps of both? Aubrey Stacey continued to ponder for some time, then he got out his monograph on old Cotton and started to work on it.

To the Royces, if anyone had been able to trace it, the transition from the one realm to the other was perceptible, if precarious. Harriet had started school again fairly happily at half-term. Andrew and Margot had got married very quietly one weekend. When told of this, Harriet was pleased.

"This makes you a real relation to me, doesn't it?" she had said to Andrew. "And us into a proper family." She had confided the news to her mascot which she generally carted around in her pocket.

"I think we ought to have a honeymoon," Andrew said to Margot, "your trip to Egypt didn't do you much good, and I've still some leave left. Where would you like to go?"

"Switzerland," said Margot without hesitation.

"We could take Harriet with us as chaperone," said Andrew, "newly married couples always took a chaperone in Jane Austen's day."

"But this isn't Jane Austen's day," said Margot, "it *isn't*, Andrew."

"No, perhaps not," said Andrew, "I've always wondered what they did, the chaperones I mean. What can we do about her then?"

"Miss Johnson did say something about a music school away somewhere in Wales in the summer holidays, and would she be fit, did I think?"

"Just the thing," said Andrew, "she's really almost as fit as a fiddle now, isn't she?"

"Switzerland's expensive," said Margot, "and the music school won't be cheap, but we could sell the Crispin Keylock statue, he's fetching quite high prices now and it would help a bit."

Andrew had agreed enthusiastically. He had never cared for that annorexic nude, as he called it, and the thought of Crispin helping to pay for their honeymoon pleased him. Now he sat comfortably beside Margot and Harriet on the sofa in preparation for Miss Cook's programme. Harriet was in what Margot called a tizzy, afraid that they might miss the beginning since Andrew insisted on waiting until the exact time advertised in order not to have to see the preceding item, which he declared would turn his stomach.

"Don't fuss," said her mother.

Harriet stole a sidelong look at her. "Well, you fussed yesterday when you thought he would make you lose your train."

"How right you are, Harriet," said Andrew, "but then you women always fuss, I suppose you can't help it."

Harriet looked quickly at her mother again, but it was all right, she was smiling and the smile was for Harriet and was almost like a wink. She gave a contented giggle, but she was still anxious. At last Andrew stopped concentrating on the second hand of his watch and switched on just as the programme was being announced, and then they each saw the strip of flower garden and Miss Cook and the house.

Andrew noted once more with affectionate approval its fine proportions and classical grace. He hoped Margot would not want to move again for a long while. He was glad that the Lotus House was their first home as man and wife.

Margot, looking at the bright small image before her, was suddenly reminded of her nightmare in Egypt for, as bright and small had been the vision at the end of that dark avenue. She remembered but no longer felt the horror of her dream. It had been a horror of vacuity. Perhaps this had always haunted her, perhaps she had always been trying to escape from it ever since her empty childhood, and always in vain, for without love there is no identity. Since Harriet's accident she had sensed this dimly. The quest and the flight (for they were one) still harried her, but there had been that moment of peaceful radiance in the midst of Andrew's absurd dance, the influence of which had never entirely deserted her. She watched the picture of the Lotus House and garden before her change now to a close-up of Miss Cook holding her pelargonium proudly aloft for all to see. Her hands, clasping the pot, were out of focus and looked too large. They were untended hands with short stubby fingers. Margot looked down involuntarily at her own hands, beautifully smooth, the nails like small very pink shells. Then she glanced at Harriet's and noticed for the first time, and with surprise, that they were prettily shaped and very like her own. She did not need to look at Andrew's — those inordinately long, very sensitive fingers — she had an odd sensation that they were as much a part of her as her own.

"Who are those three little girls on the stairway hiding behind the wisteria?" Harriet was asking.

"I can't see any little girls," said Margot.

"It must be the shadows of the leaves," said Andrew.

"Oh, look!" cried out Harriet excitedly, "There's Maisie, I'm so glad she's there, she's walking all the way down the path. Wasn't she clever to know about it?"

"I expect they decoyed her with a bit of fish," said Andrew, "cats are TV personalities, the public loves them."

Underneath the Royces, Letty sat alone in her beautiful old green and white drawing-room, the least altered room in the house, and the one she liked the best. She regretted that she was alone but knew now it was only to be expected. The crisis of Harriet's accident had drawn them all together for a short while, but that was an artificial association with no basis of natural growth, and once over, they parted again into their four separate units and really seldom met. It was not at all what Letty had at one time dreamed of, but she had come to accept it almost with amusement. She knew herself to be sentimental, but she was relieved to find she was not a coward. She had come to terms with loneliness, to which after all she was no stranger. Lately a warning physical sympton had taken her to her doctor, who had told her there was no cause for alarm, but that the time had come for her to take care. The care she had taken was for the Lotus House. She had had a session with Mr Donovan.

"I do not want it to become an institution and as far as possible I want to ensure its being looked after properly. I have no close relatives still living," she said. "What do you advise?"

It was decided that the property should go to a favourite charity on condition that they fulfilled certain obligations as to its upkeep. "But if anything should

156

happen to me while the present tenants are still in residence, I want their interests safeguarded," said Letty earnestly, and Mr Donovan said he would prepare the necessary papers. She had gone away satisfied.

It struck her now as she sat there waiting, that it was curious that it should be Cooksie in the basement that was the one who was responsible for setting all this activity in motion, that had brought producer and researcher and cameramen and interviewer and designer, and who knows how many more, into contact with her Lotus House, while she herself remained passive, a mere onlooker. But she had perhaps been more of an onlooker than anything else throughout her life — the child who enjoyed watching the sparrows on the roof more than the game — the one who stood entranced, motionless, before the doll's house — the dutiful daughter, the useful wife at home. "They also serve who only stand and wait," she had learned the sonnet at school. Milton however could not have actually done much standing and waiting, she thought, with twelve books of *Paradise Lost* to be written. Really, the only important action she had ever taken on her own was to buy the Lotus House, and how much that mattered she could not tell. The house kept its secrets. Now she felt her part in its history was over and done with, sealed up in Mr Donovan's office. She was not needed any longer, even as an onlooker. But why should one always demand of life to be needed? It was not in the bond. She could still love her drawing-room as much as she liked.

Unlike Andrew, Letty had switched on early, but she had been paying no attention to what was going on. How breathless thought was. She had traversed labyrinths of the mind in a few moments, and now she collected her wits together. As "Senior Starters" was announced, her television set gave a flicker. Perhaps after all it was as well that none of her tenants were watching with her, it was an old set and she knew she ought to replace it. *It is typical,* she thought, *that I do nothing about it because I'm used to it and it was a wedding present.* Then she caught her breath — what she was looking at was the back view of Selina's doll's house, the part that had never been seen before. It was just the right size, only a little brighter, a little further removed from reality. Where, oh where, were the Golightlys? She could not see any of them anywhere, unless that was Cooksie standing among a lot of flowers that were pretty enough but had no business to be outside the kitchen window. No, of course, Selina's doll's house was destroyed and that was Miss Janet Cook who rented the basement flat. Well, she couldn't really be bothered at her age to keep the past and the present separate any more, though she remembered clearly enough now. It was all about a blue pelargonium, but they had liked the house so much, Janet Cook has said, that they had taken a special picture of it at the end to show the whole of it to the best advantage.

There it was now, very clear, with Maisie the cat just coming round the corner. But for Letty Maisie never finished her walk, for suddenly as she gazed the whole house quivered and then splintered into a thousand shimmering dancing peacock patterns and then disappeared.